Searching for Sandra

Jane Harvey

Book Three in the Hummingbird House Series

Published by Sherman House

FIRST EDITION

Book Cover Design by Dreena Collins

ISBN: 978-1-7396126-6-5

"Friendship is born at that moment
when one person says to another:
'What! You too? I thought I was the only one."

C.S. Lewis

Characters

1968

Betty: A 29-year-old woman who owns Hummingbird House.
William: Betty's husband. They are effectively estranged.
Linda: Betty's sister-in-law.
John: Betty's brother. He lives with Linda on the top floor.
Mark: Linda and John's child.
Sandra: Betty's close friend and previous tenant.
Nigel: Sandra's brother.
Robert: Sandra's ex-boyfriend with whom she lived in the basement flat.
Arthur: A new tenant who moved into the basement flat when Robert and Sandra vacated.
Christine: Sandra's new flatmate.
Mrs Ashbury: Sandra's mother.

Now

Betty: An 83-year-old woman who owns Hummingbird House.
Jonty: Betty's tenant in Flat One.
Ben: Jonty's husband.
Mark: Linda and John's child, now grown up.
April: Betty's tenant.
Paul: April's partner.
Rosie: A former neighbour.
Joy: Rosie's partner.
Dai (David): A former tenant of Hummingbird House.
Sandra: Betty's friend. Also, Jonty's mother.

Chapter One:
Betty (1968)

'Xanadu' was blasting from the transistor. Mark sat on the rug in nothing but his nappy, bouncing up and down, laughing. Betty wasn't a fan but loved to watch her nephew's reaction each time it played on the radio: his arms flailed like a duckling, and he made that glorious, wholesome sound that only a baby can make when they descend into fits of giggles. She allowed the contagion to sweep over her until she was laughing uproariously, too; the pair of them jiggling on their bottoms, holding hands, and bobbing in an ill-timed duet.

At first, she didn't notice the banging on the door. Only afterwards did it strike her that Robert had probably been knocking for some time.

"Betty?" he called. He had opened the sitting room door and was leaning around it tentatively. She jumped. Mark flinched, too, and for a moment, she wondered if he would cry, but the fear passed over briefly, and he resumed his bouncing. Betty leaned forward, kissed his forehead for reassurance, and unfolded herself from the floor.

"Sorry," she mouthed, smiling, as she moved to the radio and turned down the volume. "Dance time for babies."

Then she walked towards him, unsure whether to reach out for a hug. She thought better of it, instead brushing her hand against his left arm and tugging at his sleeve so that he entered the room properly. His hand dropped from the door handle.

"You should lock that front door, you know," he muttered absently.

"Come in, come in. How lovely to see you! Fancy a dance?" She twirled, clapping her hands in Mark's direction. "Or tea? Come."

She gestured vaguely into the room. It was nice to have adult company.

"No, I… sorry for the interruption."

His voice was tight and small. Of course. There was a problem. He was not one to make a casual social visit. When had he ever done so in the months since he moved out from the Basement Flat? She looked at him properly for the first time. His brow was furrowed. His collar-length hair was unbrushed. He did not meet her eye, staring into the distance. She half-turned back into the room, checking on Mark again. Not that he could have gone anywhere. But she looked, nonetheless. She had to.

"What is it?"

There was silence for a beat.

"It's Sandra," he said. "Have you… you haven't seen her, have you? Recently?"

She shook her head. They both stood still for a moment, eyes locked. As they did, it struck her that this might be it. One of those moments that happens to other people. A pivotal point. Something serious.

And a weight descended on her from above. A peculiar sensation falling from her crown, across her face, her shoulders, then down her arms. The tingle. The heaviness of it Afterwards, she would recall it and be able to feel it anew.

"She's missing," he said.

Chapter Two:
Betty (1968)

She was sitting at the table, scribbling on the back of an envelope, when Arthur rapped on the sitting room door. She knew his knock. Not that Linda or John usually knocked these days, so really, he was the only one who did so. Even though the house was notionally split into units, the reality of her babysitting Mark and being in the same building as her brother and sister-in-law meant there was inevitably a lot of to-ing and fro-ing between Betty, Linda and John. Knocking was a pleasantry that was long gone. They had an unusual set-up. But it worked.

Still, Arthur's tap was rhythmical and the same every time. Ra-ta-tat-tat. Pause. Ra-ta-tat-tat-tat-tat – usually followed by a singsong, 'Helloooo!'

She smiled to herself, noting but concurrently attempting to ignore the way her own heartbeat sped up in conjunction with his knocking.

"Come in," she called.

He swung the door open and jumped into the room sideways, jazz hands wide and shimmying, legs akimbo.

"Ah, darn it. The one time you don't have pop music blaring."

She chuckled. "Attempting to impress me with a Pan's People routine, were you?"

"I've been planning that entrance all day."

All day? Had he been thinking about visiting her all day? She took in his slim but broad frame and his sandy hair. She was surprised to see him wearing checked, tailored shorts. He had a slight tan to his complexion, she noted. It emphasised his green eyes.

"If you'd have come a couple of hours ago, you'd have caught Mark and me dancing to Dave Dee, Beaky, Mick and Tich." She fumbled a little as she listed them. "Oh, and Dozy."

"Of course," he said. "Mustn't forget Dozy." He nodded with mock seriousness.

"Anyway, what can I do for you?" She started to stand. "Are you staying for tea?"

"No, no. Don't get up. I just wanted to give you a garden update."

"Oh yes?"

He walked towards her and started to pull out a chair but then hesitated. He leant down on the back of it, gripping the wood, and remained standing. She noticed how smooth his skin looked— the tiny, wispy blond hairs on the back of his hands.

"It's much better now. The water has receded substantially. It's more a pond on the lawn than a generalised flooding. You'll have seen it, I imagine. So I spoke to my friend Jim – remember I mentioned him? But he reckons we should give it at least another month; then, he'll come around and check it out. See about putting some slabs down and whether we need new grass."

"I should think we do. It's like a rugby pitch out there, isn't it?"

He nodded. "Yes, but slightly better than I thought… than we thought. The damage is a little less than I imagined. To my mind, at least."

Betty glanced down at the table and her scrawl on the envelope.

"That was such a peculiar day, wasn't it?"

"Raindrops like golf balls and the darkest sky I've ever seen." He shook his head.

He was right. The light had been extraordinary during the storm. For almost 24 hours, it had hardly lifted above twilight. The air had felt heavy and thick until the showers began and pelted them with a volley of rain and even unseasonal hail. Saharan dust fall thunderstorms, they said. Extraordinary.

She had been sitting at this very table when the weather broke. She and Sandra discussing William and how he had not been to see Betty since he had started to rent his flat away for work about six weeks earlier. She remembered it vividly. The conversation. Sandra's quiet reassurance; the undeniable knowledge that they lived apart, now; the guilt Betty felt that she didn't mind. And the light within the warm, thick air. Then Arthur, her new tenant, bursting in just ten minutes later to tell her the garden was flooding, with water already rising up against the back door of the Basement Flat.

"It was a Monday, wasn't it? Was it two weeks ago?"

"Three," he corrected. "It was three weeks yesterday. 1st July."

"Was it really? Are you sure?"

"Certain."

She dropped her pencil onto the table; she hadn't noticed she'd been holding it all this time. "Damn. That's even longer than I thought."

Three weeks? Had it been three whole weeks since she'd seen Sandra? She rubbed her hands across her temple and buried her fingers into her eyes. That was a long time. Anything could have happened in that amount of time. Anything.

"What's— is everything all right?"

She glanced up to see him leaning forward, a pinch of concern between his eyebrows.

"If it's… I hope you won't think me indelicate, but if it's the cost you're concerned about. Well, Jim's a good fellow. He'll do us a deal. And besides, I don't mind throwing in a few bob to help. After all, I'm the main person who benefits from the space."

She stared at him for a moment, unable to process what he was saying. Then she gave a short hard laugh.

"Ha! Sorry." She shook her head. "That's very kind of you, but I'm not worried about that. Truth be told, I've hardly considered it. But the garden would benefit from a tidy-up, anyway. I'm sure it'll be fine."

"Oh, right." A hint of a blush rose from his collar towards his face. "Sorry if I offended you. I just thought you looked…."

"Sit down, why don't you?" She waved one hand at the chair. "It's not that. My friend Sandra. You know, the one who was here that day? Do you remember?"

He sat. She had forgotten how small the table was. How close this would bring him to her. "The one who used to live downstairs. In the basement. Before me."

"That's right." He had paid attention, then.

"The cheeky one." He grinned. Sandra had made an impression, it seemed. Now it was her turn to blush. She didn't respond.

"She's… no one has seen her in a while. So I've been trying to determine the last time I heard from or saw her. And I think it was then: July 1st. I think it was during the Saharan storms."

"And you're worried, I take it? You'd usually hear from her more often?"

She nodded vigorously. "Much more often."

Arthur rested his chin on the palm of his right hand. The table was a little low, and he was curled awkwardly, a man-child in his shorts at a school desk, as he considered her words.

"Tell me all about it," he said. "Let's see if we can work this out together."

*

Arthur had ripped open the envelope with a butter knife and drawn a neat table on the clean paper within. He had occasionally prompted her with questions, but he mostly listened in silence, noting down anything that he thought relevant. And now they had their timeline. It had taken just twenty minutes.

He held the paper before him at arm's length.

"Three weeks and one day since you saw her. Eighteen days since your friend Robert did – he's an old boyfriend of hers, but they are still in the same social circle. Friendly enough.

"No one answered when you went around her flat twelve or thirteen days ago. You didn't think much of it. She has no telephone, so you don't talk that way. You thought she was in good spirits when you saw her – when *we* saw her last, though she didn't say much as it was all about… what did you say? Your family?"

Betty smiled. The conversation had been entirely focussed on the peculiar state of her marriage – but she'd not told Arthur that. She nodded.

"Quiet then. But fine, you thought. She's not always one for a routine and can be spontaneous. But she has little cash to splash and hadn't mentioned going away.

Robert came around today – this afternoon? Worried about her because her flatmate said she'd not been seen for many days – details vague but enough to cause a degree of alarm. Right so far?"

"Right." She sunk down, resting her head on her arms. "Not much of a friend, am I?"

"I don't know about that. I'm friends with some top blokes I've not seen in months. It happens."

But she used to see her every day when Sandra lived here. How could things have shifted so quickly?

"Her flatmate is called Christine," Sandra added, pleased to remember something concrete. "She works at the dressmaker's on the high street."

"Good. Anyone else important in her life? Parents?"

Betty shook her head. "Her mother lives in Sussex. But I rather doubt she'd go there. They… aren't close."

He made a note. "We should check, though, to be sure. You never know—"

"Nigel!" she cried out. "How could I be so daft? We need to ask Nigel. Her brother."

Chapter Three:
Jonty (Now)

Dai was sitting on the wall outside the house as if he had never left. His t-shirt was tight, biceps larger than they had been in a while. Belly, too, Jonty noted; it sat neat and gently rounded above the low waistline of tracksuit bottoms. Comforting. And he was still stunning, of course.

It had been a few months since he had seen Dai – at least six months since he had left. A six-month period that had been much kinder than the preceding one, it seemed.

The sharp point of a tattoo jutted out from beneath the fabric on his left hand-side. A new smaller piece now decorated his right forearm. An inscription of sorts.

He was poised, still – hands clasped together as he grinned broadly at Jonty's arrival.

"About time," he called.

"Some of us started at nine, actually. I'm just back from a run to the dump."

Jonty bent towards him to give him a hug, which for some reason, Dai took to be a high five, then a fist bump. As if Jonty had ever given one of those.

They grappled in the space, limbs smacking awkwardly as though fumbling in some pseudo martial art. Jonty laughed.

"Tea?"

He walked the short path to the front door and jangled his pockets to locate the key, catching a whiff of the rosemary growing in a pot outside the bay window.

"A quick one. Summon up some energy before we get to work."

"Get *back* to work, in my case." Jonty tapped his chest. "Nine a.m. Nine."

"OK, old man. You've made your point. Don't worry; I'll pull my weight."

They entered the hallway. Bright. Clean. Neutral. There was a faint scent of cleaning products hanging in the air, and Jonty could sense the usual warmth of the house, which seemed, each year, to latch onto the summer and hold it tight – gathering it up, somehow making the building one or two degrees warmer than the outside. Day or night. Or so it felt to him, at least.

And he could hear a radio playing upstairs, mixed with occasional, gentle thuds as Paul and April shifted furniture and boxes – preparing to move into the top flat of Hummingbird House together.

*

"I don't have any biscuits."

"Ben still on his health kick? I wish I had that kind of dedication."

"Actually, I don't have any biscuits because I ate them all last night." He laughed. "But yes, he is. Still jogs most days. And he is encouraging me to eat less meat."

Jonty slapped his belly, which was not exactly trim but was at least smaller than it had been. At 54, he was finding it harder to keep the weight off, though he had always been on the slight side.

He opened the back window, and Oxo slinked in instantly, having navigated a tightrope of a shortcut across a flat roof and a window ledge to get there. He gave a sharp mew and then skipped straight to Dai, who had made himself comfortable on the sofa.

"Ah, my precious. You haven't forgotten me, then." Dai's eyes lit up.

"As if he would. You've always been a favourite."

"You're looking a bit thin, mate."

Dai's voice was low as tenderly he stroked the entire length of the cat, who leant into his touch, body tensed forward and eyes in ecstatic half-moons. It was true. Oxo had also lost weight, and his coat was patchy these days, his eyes and nose prone to watering. But they were both getting older, it seemed; Oxo was at least fifteen now, possibly more, so it was no wonder he was starting to look less sleek. Jonty didn't like to think what this might mean and set himself back on the more comfortable job of making the tea.

By the time he returned from the small kitchen, Oxo had settled in a neat circle on Dai's lap where he lounged; head flopped against the top of the sofa, shoes kicked off.

"Don't get too comfy."

"Don't worry; I'm just enjoying the company. And the house. I mean, I do love living alone. The flat is perfect, but…." He trailed off.

"There's no place like home." Jonty placed the tea on the small table next to the arm of the sofa.

"Ha!" Dai replied. "I suppose not. It's probably the place I've lived the longest. So sort of home, I suppose."

Of course, there was more to it than that. The history. The memories. But Jonty left it unsaid and nodded instead.

"How's work?" he asked. "Still… doing accountancy-type things?"

Dai smiled. "Yes, accountancy-type things. Senior Client Accountant now. Not that there are many people to have seniority over. It's good of them after I had all that time off."

"I'm sure you're worth your weight in gold."

Jonty's phone pinged with a message. He took it from his pocket, glanced at the screen and then wiggled his mobile vaguely in Dai's direction.

"April is chasing us."

Dai gave a small salute and then swigged back his tea.

"Tell her David says, '*Righto!*'" he said between gulps.

*

Paul had lined the corridor of the middle floor with boxes, each the same size, and labelled clearly (room, followed by content) in a uniform capitalised script. The cartons were placed in clusters, grouped by destination, and each pushed back against the wall or one another, tessellating together, perfectly neat.

April came out onto the landing as she heard them take the stairs, and Jonty grinned to himself as she dropped the tea towel she was holding into the nearest box (BATHROOM: MEDICINE AND FIRST AID) and bounced over. She went straight to Dai and gave him a broad hug.

"Long time no see," she said into his curly hair. She stepped back to take him in, holding him at arm's length. "Looking good. Glad to see you haven't slipped back into your grungy ways."

"Where's the boss?"

"Which one? Betty, or my better half?"

"Either, I guess."

"Well, Betty is on the top floor inspecting the bathroom tiling, I believe, and Paul is busily wrapping ornaments in excessive quantities of bubble wrap. His eco principles go out that window when it comes to packing." She stepped back. "Thank you for coming. I hope it's not... you know."

She shrugged. They all knew.

"Yeah, it's fine. I'm fine."

"Good," she said. "Good."

Dai's flat had been empty since he moved out into the newly built flat that April, herself, owned. It was a convoluted arrangement but seemed to suit them, and it had prompted their landlady, Betty, into a period of renovation and decoration that was timely – perhaps even overdue. New doors on the kitchen cupboards. A fresh coat of paint. And the bathroom was completely gutted and made over.

She'd even replaced the tatty carpet on both flights of stairs.

At first, Jonty had wondered if Betty would take the flat herself. After all, her basement space was the smallest of the lot. But she gave a Mona Lisa smile each time he mentioned it and made vague comments about it being a home meant for two. Besides, it was a lot of stairs for someone her age to navigate, she said; until one day, it became clear that Paul and April would be moving in, vacating flats two and three and setting up a home together. It was the obvious next step, really, once he heard the news. The time it had taken for Dai's flat to be ready and then the few months of work at Hummingbird House meant they'd been together ten months or so by the time it was ready and were settled into a relationship yet still clearly doted on one another. So it was serendipity.

He wondered who would move into the middle floor once they had vacated. Betty seemed in no hurry to let those rooms, either. And he was in no rush for new neighbours, so it wasn't a topic he raised very often. There had been enough drama in Hummingbird House in the last year. The idea of new neighbours was not an appealing one.

Chapter Four: Betty (Now)

Rosie and Joy had moved into their new home, across the other side of the park, about a week earlier. There was a time when she wouldn't have blinked an eyelid at the prospect of such a walk – after all, she had done it many times, perhaps thousands over the years. But this week, she had to find the right moment to make the trip to see them. A day when her knees were cooperating, and the weather didn't put her off. Too hot, and she would find herself out of breath. Too chilly, and she'd feel cold for the rest of the day.

She slipped on some flat shoes, picked up her bag (laden with scones) and went out the front door, checking behind her to ensure it had shut fast.

When was the last time she had walked through the park? Two, perhaps three weeks? How did days pass by so quickly? There was a time when she would have trekked through it almost every day. She marked each spring by the bloom of the daffodils; she loved to watch the summer bedding plants bursting into colour. But that was years ago now. She had even spent several afternoons sunbathing on the grass, decades earlier, oiled in tanning lotion, dozing on a blanket while William read beside her – before they bought Hummingbird House.

She didn't know Joy well, but Rosie had been around the house frequently since they had first met at a house barbecue last August. She was friendly with Paul and April: a cheerful, open sort with a love of art and gardening. Green fingers aside, she reminded her very much of how Sandra had been when they first met. Bold in opinions and curious – one might even say nosy – in her directness. Not that April was exactly retiring, either. Perhaps this was just the way young women were these days. Maybe Sandra was simply ahead of her time.

Now Rosie and Joy had sold their flat and moved a little across town, taking a terraced house, which she was told needed some work but was full of potential. Joy worked in property in some regard and had an eye for these things. Not that they had much time to get it sorted. Joy's belly seemed to grow bigger before her eyes each time Betty saw her.

As she approached the exit of the park, she saw it. Her old doctor's surgery. And she shook her head to drive away her own painful memories of pregnancy. Even now, all these years later, it could buckle her. Even now. But not today. Today she had scones, positive thoughts and the promise of a baby to visit in the future. She was sure of it.

*

Joy was wearing a bikini top and some sort of wrapped scarf as a skirt when she opened the front door. Betty jumped slightly at the sight of her: torso huge and tight, with white snail trails of bright stretch marks against her dark skin, rising from the band of her skirt towards her belly button. She had cropped her afro short and wrapped her hairline with a wide headband.

"Betty!" she cried, glancing at her watch. "Wow, I lost track of time. But it's lovely to have you here."

Joy stepped back and held the door open wide for her to step inside. Betty tried not to stare at her tummy, which protruded into the hallway, making it hard for her to pass without brushing against her.

Rosie appeared from a door on the right.

"Hi!" She glanced at Joy. "Good God, woman. You're practically naked. You'll be giving poor Betty a heart attack." She walked down the corridor and automatically took Betty's bag from her arm.

"Gah! I know, I know. But it's boiling. Isn't it boiling? I just can't get comfortable."

"It's certainly a nice day," Betty replied. It wasn't any warmer than usual, but it seemed churlish to point this out.

"I'll go and find a wrap or something. Don't worry." She closed the door and skipped straight up the stairs, barefoot and surprisingly agile for her size.

"Come into the kitchen. It's the least like a building site. Which is not saying much… Anyway, I don't want to dwell on our chaos. It just makes me stressed. What I'm dying to hear about are the latest comings and goings in the house."

Chapter Five: Jonty (Now)

"You could move into one of the flats on the middle floor, couldn't you? I know you didn't want the top floor, but number two could be nice?"

He sat with Betty at her kitchen table as they shelled fresh peas together. It was almost therapeutic – it took him back to his childhood. Doing the same with Nan. He enjoyed the soft plink of the peas as they hit the empty saucepan.

"You are nothing if not persistent, Jonty."

He smiled. "I just think it's a shame that you have the smallest and darkest space in the building. You should enjoy the house. You've earnt it… literally."

"I do enjoy the house. I love this flat. It's my home and holds some special memories for me."

"Well, it's up to you, but –"

"Yes, it is," she interrupted. Her tone edged towards forceful. Enough to tell him to drop it. "I have no plans to move. Ever."

He glanced over and raised his eyebrows.

"Even if I have to add a stair lift or put in some sort of dumb waiter for you to send food down to me," she added.

"Fair enough," he said. "Sorry for interfering… now, tell me all about the girls' new place. Fabulous, I expect."

Betty paused. "In places, yes. But they have a lot of work on their hands. The previous owners had made a start but apparently found they had bitten off more than they could chew, so the hallway is almost finished, lovely and bright, with original tiles, and the kitchen only needs a new floor. The downstairs toilet is certainly liveable. Though naturally, none of it passes muster for Rosie. I gather she'd tear the whole thing out and start again if she had the chance."

"Poor Joy," he said, softly shaking his head – but smiling.

"Oh, don't worry. I think common sense is overruling her design aspirations at the moment. She's putting a quick coat of white paint everywhere this week."

"That's a relief."

"Cerise pink in the toilet, though."

"Naturally." He chuckled. He'd only been inside Rosie and Joy's old home once, but it was seared in his memory – packed with plants and paintings. It was a kaleidoscope.

"And the garden is wonderful, of course. It's what sold it to them. She's managed to salvage and relocate a whole row of planters and pots from the old place, which are bursting with produce on the patio. There's an established apple tree in the middle and some soft fruits at the back. They tell me the weeds were knee-high when they arrived, but you'd never know it now – that was the first thing she tackled. In fact, they gave me a bag of Bramleys. The first crop of the season. Small and early, but they look lovely. How handy are you with a peeler?"

"You can rely on me, Betty. Assuming you'll be paying me in crumble, that is."

*

"Still no answer?" Ben was walking briskly about the flat after returning from his run. He pumped his arms in an exaggerated motion and marched with his knees up high. He wore lycra cycling shorts and socks pulled high, though thankfully a loose-fitting t-shirt that offered some dignity.

"No." Jonty frowned. "But I suppose it's not unheard of for mum to be elusive."

Ben stopped striding and came to a standstill in front of him, marching on the spot. The warm smell of his damp skin hovered about him.

"How long's it been now? Since you spoke?"

"Eight days."

"Eight?" Ben exclaimed. He stopped walking and took a step closer. "I didn't realise… Eight. Are you sure?"

He nodded. "Yeah, it was the Sunday before last that I spoke to her. I remember as we'd been down to see Betty. Roast pork."

"Sunday roast. Yeah." His eyes glazed at the thought of it. "God, so it must be over a week. You don't think… should we…" He trailed off as if saying the words aloud might cause alarm.

"Visit? Check on her?" He sighed. "No, I'm not that concerned. She did say there was some sort of street party going on soon, but she was vague about the details. She's probably tied up creating a giant painting. Making bunting."

Ben snorted. "I'm not sure Sandra is the bunting type."

"True. More likely, she'd been arrested for including willies in the mural or something."

"*It's only the human body, darling. Nothing to be embarrassed about*," Jonty mimicked.

"Talking of which, this human body in front of me probably needs to get out of these clothes." Jonty grabbed Ben's upper arms and squeezed them.

"Oh yes?" He raised his eyebrows. "What exactly are you suggesting?" He glanced down to where Jonty's fingers circled his biceps.

"Uh, sadly, I am suggesting that I can smell you from here. Sorry." He gave him a firm pat and then leaned forward to kiss Ben's cheek. "No offence."

"Offence taken… But I shall go to resolve this forthwith."

*

He was helping April to move the sofa from one side of the room to the other. Not far, but it was clearly a job for two. She had told Jonty she wanted to do it while Paul was at work, as they had mutually decided on the original spot, but now she had thought better of it and wanted to face the windows. Typically April.

"If I do it while he's out, it's a fait accompli. I know that's childish. And sneaky. But honestly, he'd want to think over it for another week, and I just can't bear it. It's darker than the flats downstairs, being this high, with the small windows. I want to get all the light I can."

"I wonder how he'll take it. Don't let on that I was your accomplice." Jonty sat down on the sofa in its new spot. He had to admit she was right. Although they had only been in the place hours, it seemed, somehow it already felt cosy and dressed.

"Thank goodness for summer holidays," she said, sitting beside him. "I could never have mobilised us to finish this during term time. It's bad enough doing it while I'm juggling planning and paperwork, and he's at the office. I mean, between his procrastination and my disorganisation, we aren't exactly a smooth machine."

"I don't think you're disorganised in the slightest." He turned to look at her, surprised.

"Really?" Her face lit up. "I am going to be dining out on that for weeks. My sister will think it's hilarious."

"A bit… spontaneous, maybe. And excitable. But not disorganised."

April threw her head back and gave a hearty laugh. "I sound like a chaotic nightmare!"

He patted her knee. "Nooo! But you get things done. You chivvy us all along. I've never seen Paul move so quickly. He was in the flat for two years before he even put a picture up. And I know that's not from disorganisation, but still… you're good for him. You're good for each other. You balance one another out."

She grinned. "And I'm the best judge of where the furniture should go, though, right?"

*

An hour later, he was clutching an empty coffee mug and telling her about his mum. April leant forward, brows down. Every time he told her a new detail or anecdote, she simply said: "Wow!" softly. He told her about how she had painted her front door bright green, blatantly ignoring the fact that she lived in an ancient cottage in a conservation area. She'd blocked all words of advice from the neighbours and disregarded letters through the door until one day, she was visited by a 'very pleasant young man' who managed – miraculously – to talk sense into her. Goodness knows how. But he left her house with a newly acquired appreciation for rooibos tea and the apparently half-decent sketch of a robin she'd been working on when he arrived.

"She sounds amazing. I can't believe I haven't met her."

"She was here last summer, around the end of August. But not for long. She gets restless. I'm not sure where you were. It was the day after the barbecue, remember?"

"Remember?" She slapped his arm gently. "Of course I do. That's when Paul and I got together."

"Of course. Well, she came down the next day. So perhaps you were otherwise engaged."

"No comment," she said. She leant forward and gestured towards his mug, which he passed to her. "You went up to her for Christmas, didn't you?" She stood. "Another coffee?"

He had seen her that Christmas, April was right. And she had been as lively and mischievous as ever.

"Oh, no. I must get going. I must do some work at some point today."

"Ah yes, buying and selling your goodies. Please do keep an eye out for a dresser for me, won't you?"

"As long as you promise to mention it to Paul. Being in cahoots about moving your sofa is one thing, but I don't want to make a habit of it."

She nodded. "I will; I will… But tell me, you're saying she's AWOL, your mum. Are you worried?"

"A little. Perhaps. But I try not to. I learned a long time ago that it is impossible to live in a perpetual state of fear. And unhelpful."

"Really?" She called over to him as she moved towards the sink. "Is she that bad?"

"She can be." Yes. She could.

"Not exactly out of character, then. To go quiet or wander off. Has she done this before?"

"Oh yes," he said. "She certainly has."

Chapter Six:
Betty (1968)

A scrap of paper holding Nigel's address had been clamped to the fridge door by a magnet since Sandra first mentioned moving out. Held tight under a little wooden owl with a thermometer that didn't seem to work.

Betty recalled the feeling that hit her as Sandra said the words aloud. She knew it was coming. Yet it still stung. Robert had already left, and managing the rent was too much for Sandra to do alone.

And logical as it was, Betty doubted this was the only reason. Sandra was far from a classic romantic, but Betty knew the relationship break-up had hit her hard. The couple were still talking, or civil at least, and there had been only one large row. But this had bruised her badly, and it wasn't her way to wallow. Or stagnate. Moving on and being around more people was a natural response for Sandra. Precisely the sort of thing she would do.

"What if I… I could lower the rent?" Betty had said, clutching her empty tea cup.

Nigel had looked over sharply with a frown. He had sat silently on the opposite sofa, nodding, as

Sandra had been talking about finding a shared house with other young women. She'd made it sound hedonistic.

"That's not really a solution," Sandra replied.

"No, little sis. It's really not." His voice was firm.

A memory of her mother chastising her for befriending her tenants popped into her head. She knew they were both right. She needed the income simply to keep on top of maintaining and tidying up the house.

But she didn't want Sandra to go.

"It's not just the money. Look, if I really wanted to, I could get a steadier income. I could do more waitressing for Charles – you know, the chap I worked for last month? Probably even get more shifts at College. But it's not just that. I think it's time."

Embarrassingly, Betty felt her eyes prick with tears. Sandra couldn't even see her face but stepped over from where she'd been standing in the kitchen area, walking behind the chair where Betty sat and placing her hands on her shoulders. Betty stared down at the G-Plan table with its polished teak surface and curved edges.

"When?" Betty asked.

"Listen, you're the only reason I've hesitated about leaving at all. I'd probably have done a runner at midnight by now if it was anyone else."

"She's not kidding, darling," Nigel said.

"I'm thinking a couple of months? To be honest, we'd already vaguely talked about getting somewhere more central before things went all to cock. But I need time to find somewhere and to get bloody Rob to pick up the last of his tat." Her voice wobbled at the mention of his name.

"I expect an invitation to the housewarming," Nigel said.

"Housewarming? You'll get to see it plenty of times when you're carrying boxes for me, brother dear."

"I hope you don't end up miles away," Betty said.

"Could be just the incentive you need to finally learn to drive," Sandra muttered, close to her left ear. She jumped at the unexpected intimacy. "Don't worry. You won't shake me off that easily."

"Nor me." Nigel pulled out a pen from his jacket pocket. "Get me some paper, Sandy; I want to ensure this one has my number."

Betty turned and watched as Sandra walked back towards the kitchen table and tore the edge from the front page of the Daily Mirror. Her thick yellow woollen tights had a small hole on the left leg. Her hair was flat and unwashed. She looked small. Delicate.

She called over to them. "Besides, it'll probably be six months yet. You know me, I have these ideas, but I can be a bit of a cabbage when it comes to organisation."

"You said it, Sand."

*

As it happened, it was only about three weeks later that Sandra was offered a room. The property was owned by Christine's uncle, and her previous flatmate had moved to Scotland suddenly to be with family when her mother had fallen ill. The room was empty. The flat was warm and secure. Christine was easy-going but sensible. It was the perfect solution.

Sandra had been almost shy when she came to tell her.

"Honestly, please don't think I lied when I said it would be months. It wasn't some wicked scheme or something. This just happened." She was talking quickly, a little louder than necessary. Was she nervous? Excited? "Christine used to be a student at College. She even knows Robert through music. But she's not… she doesn't smoke or anything. She's more one for a chinwag over a glass of Blue Nun. And she works. She's a dressmaker."

Sandra was leaning forward through the doorway of the sitting room, one hand gripping the doorframe. Betty could see the uneven application of her makeup, caked in places. Her clothes – or perhaps her skin – had a faint smell of dampness or mildew.

"Look, it's fine. I'm glad for you." She almost meant it. Wanted to.

"Are you sure?"

"Of course. I've made my peace with it." She wrapped her arms around Sandra's waist suddenly and was relieved when she finally let go of the door frame and did the same in return.

*

Now, Arthur sat on the floor in the hallway beside her as Betty made the call, his short, stocky legs bent at the knees as he rested awkwardly against the wall with its new scrubbable vinyl wallpaper. Betty perched on the small pouffe that sat in the hallway for the rare occasion that she used the telephone. Usually, to call William. And now, here she sat with a man he had never met.

"Three weeks. Well, just over," she repeated. "And her flatmate told Robert she hadn't seen her in days, but honestly, that was all a bit vague. Robert… well, he's not the most direct or clearest of communicators."

The phone line crackled.

"Quite," Nigel replied. "Listen, I'm going to need a moment to reflect on this and figure out exactly when I saw her last myself. I really don't think it was that lo— But it strikes me that we need to have a dekko of her flat and get the details from Christine ourselves. From the horse's mouth."

"Yes, that's what I was thinking… Though, to be honest, I was harbouring a secret hope that I'd speak to you, and you'd laugh and say she'd been with you this whole time."

"With me? Goodness no. She wouldn't be seen dead in our neck of the woods."

"Right," she murmured. "When shall we go around?"

"It's obviously too late now. I can usually get out prompt on a Wednesday. What about tomorrow, after work? Or will you have… thingamy? Your nephew?"

"Mark," she said.

"Yes, sorry. Will you be looking after Mark?"

"No, I can be there." She looked over to Arthur to see his reaction. "I can meet you at Christine's tomorrow, about 5.30?"

Arthur nodded vigorously.

"Well, hopefully, I'll be there just before."

"Great, see you then. Thank you."

"On the contrary, little sis. Thank you for being a good friend to my wayward sister."

*

Arthur parked up confidently on the street close to Christine's flat. Betty was glad to arrive. Cool as it was, his cream Mini rattled and spat occasionally while he drove, and she felt peculiarly vulnerable sitting in its small bubble shell as if she was too close to the road.

She had taken her time choosing her outfit that afternoon, telling herself she wanted to strike the right tone with Christine, and of course, there was the weather to factor in. Eventually, she had settled on a light cotton shift of blue gingham with white shorts beneath. Yet, she still found herself sweating and shifting in her seat – painfully aware of Arthur's proximity to her as he sat in his work clothes, tie still around his neck but loose. Short sleeves rolled up to his elbows. Top button undone. What would William think of her gadding about with Arthur like this? Well, the truth was he'd probably never know. Not from any deliberate deception on her part – more because it was unlikely they'd talk long enough for the topic to arise.

Arthur lit a cigarette as he got out of the car, and by the time they meandered to the front door, Nigel could be seen just a few yards away, approaching from the other direction.

"Great timing!" he called.

She smiled and paused until he was six or seven feet away.

"This is Arthur," she said, gesturing. "He's moved into the basement and offered me a lift."

Momentarily, Nigel raised his eyebrows. Just briefly. She caught the look that hit his face and how he rectified it in an instant. He reached out his hand.

"Nigel. It's my vagabond sister who has caused all this fuss."

Arthur held the cigarette between his lips and wiped his hand on his trousers before holding it out in return.

"He's met Sandra and was keen to help." Betty found herself explaining. "Luckily for me, as it's a walk and a bus journey to get here, which is not much fun in the rush hour."

"You drove Betty here?" Nigel glanced at his watch.

Arthur put out his cigarette under his shoe in one swift movement, swivelling his hips: like he was dancing. Then he gestured vaguely in the direction of the car.

"Mini," he said. "Surprisingly nippy. And I popped off from work a bit early to ensure we weren't late."

"You did?" Betty turned to look at him. He didn't meet her eye, though he gave a shy grin.

"It's no bother. I can make up the time tomorrow."

"Good chap," Nigel said, patting Arthur on the upper arm. "Good chap… anyway, let's do this, shall we?"

He turned towards the building and skipped lightly up the three small steps to the front door, ringing the bell in an instant.

Chapter Seven: Betty (1968)

Christine answered the door after the third ring, barefoot and tanned. She gave a small jump at the sight of them.

"Oh, God. What… has something happened?" Her hands went to her face.

"No, dear girl. No, no." Nigel stepped forward and put one arm loosely about her shoulders. "Nothing to get your knickers in a twist about. We just want to chat."

"Oh, thank goodness. It's just when I saw you all, well…." She wiped her eyes, which were suddenly damp, then dropped her hands back to her sides. Betty was flooded with guilt. Of course, she would think the worst. "Come in," she said. "Come in."

*

The flat was small, with a pink carpet that had seen better days and textured green wallpaper, torn in places – but the two women had clearly made an effort to turn it into a home. A huge beanbag was in one corner, and a framed geometric print was on the wall above the sofa. Opposite was the same cerise and yellow oil painting that had hung in the basement at Hummingbird House: three abstract naked people dancing. Sandra's own work. It struck Betty as odd that she would hang it here when she had been so adamant that it was Robert, not her, who had wanted it on display in their last home.

The three guests squished awkwardly onto the two-seater sofa, each vigorously asserting that they were fine and didn't need to use the bean bag.

Christine didn't offer them a drink but sat straight down in the only chair and leant forward, clearly anticipating an interview of sorts.

It was Arthur who spoke first.

"Thank you for inviting us in. This must be rather peculiar for you. It's just that Betty and…." He hesitated, then seemed to retrieve the name, "And Nigel are very concerned to establish the whereabouts of Sandra. I am, too, of course. I met her once a few weeks back. With Betsy."

Betsy. He called her Betsy. No one ever did that. Christine nodded briskly but didn't speak.

"That was over three weeks ago now. The Saharan storms, you know? Well, none of us has seen her since. Right?" Arthur looked to Nigel for confirmation, who gave a sombre nod, eyes closed. "I… come to think of it, maybe I'm not the person to be talking, actually. Sorry. Like I said, I'm just here as moral support. For Betsy."

"On the contrary, dear boy. You are doing just fine," Nigel muttered.

"OK, well." Arthur took a breath and continued. "Her ex-boyfriend came around this week and said he's not seen her in two or two and a half weeks either. All very odd. So that just leaves you…."

Betty sat perfectly still on the sofa in the middle of the two men. She could feel her knees against them – Nigel sat back, his usual loose-limbed, slightly gangly pose, with one leg brushing against hers. He was resting his head casually in his hand, cradling his jaw between finger and thumb as he leant on the arm of the sofa. Arthur, on the other hand, was taut, leaning forward, energised. His knee pushed hard into hers, and she could feel his fingers against the cotton of her skirt as he rubbed his thigh occasionally while he spoke. It was an odd juxtaposition as if their roles were the wrong way around. And there was Betty – Betsy – stuck in the middle.

"Yes. But I told Robert. It's been three weeks since I saw her as well. Twenty days. It was the 3rd of July."

"Really?" Betty asked. It was the first time she had spoken. "Robert implied you weren't sure. Are you certain?"

Christine frowned. "Of course I am."

"Sorry, I didn't mean that to sound accusatory. I'm just worried and keen to get this right."

"I know it was the 3rd because it was my birthday. She cooked me tea. Then the next day, I rose early and went to work, and I've not seen her since."

Nigel leant forward. "Little sis, what did you say Robert told you about how long it had been since he'd seen her himself?"

Betty felt a peculiar sensation, like pins and needles across her face. "Eighteen days."

"When was that?"

"Yesterday." She spoke quietly.

"Nineteen, then." He paused. "But that means...."

"Robert was the last person to see her," Arthur finished for him.

*

It seemed odd to be sat at her own table while someone else cooked, but somehow Arthur had persuaded her that this was the right thing to do. It was almost 7 p.m. by the time they left Christine's, and she hadn't even considered dinner beforehand. On the other hand, Arthur assured her that he had sausages that needed to be used up, and as she had a lot on her mind, this was the ideal solution.

So she was sitting, a glass of sherry before her (which he'd also brought up from the basement), while he was beating a batter mixture for the toad-in-the-hole. The double doors to the kitchen were open, and she watched as he confidently cradled the bowl and attacked the mixture with gusto, having just poured in some more milk.

He paused for breath and laughed as he realised she was watching him.

"I shouldn't have declined your offer of a pinny." He indicated the splatter on his shirt and upper legs. Luckily he had removed his tie already.

"You know," she said. "I don't think I have ever had a meal made for me by a man."

"I should think you have. All the best chefs are men, aren't they?"

"Are you calling yourself a chef?"

"No, I'm calling myself one of the best chefs, actually."

She smiled and raised her glass. "I hope so."

He continued to beat but with less aggression than earlier.

"It was my mother. It was an endless stream of baked goods and home cooking in our household." He was a little out of breath as he spoke but continued nonetheless. "The kitchen opened straight into the dining area, and I used to sit watching her as she faced me while she prepped. Better than television, not that we had one. I think I sort of absorbed it all without really realising it. And then, as we got older, she insisted we all learn five basic meals that we could do without the need for a recipe. My three sisters and me. She made no exception for me." He paused, hugging the bowl to his torso. "I suppose that's a bit peculiar now I come to think of it. But we didn't question it at the time."

"Maybe unusual, but certainly handy."

"For impressing the landlady, you mean."

He took the bowl over and placed it on the countertop to rest. Betty felt the familiar sensation of heat rising from her collar as blushes swamped her.

"Usually, I'd leave that for at least an hour, but I don't suppose you're keen on eating at 10 p.m., so we shall have to make do."

She watched him pull the tray from the oven, which he had previously dotted with lard. He tipped all six sausages in and shook the tray to cover them. They spat angrily in the fat until he slid the pan back into the oven.

"Can you sit for a minute?" she asked. "I feel guilty."

"Just a moment. When they are browned off, I'll add the batter, and we can talk. Unless you want vegetables? I was just going to keep it simple and do some Bisto."

"You've done plenty. I can live without vegetables… but let me get you a drink. I think there's some beer tucked away. Would that do?"

"I wouldn't say no."

She stood and walked towards him. The beer was in the cupboard where he was leaning. He grinned as she approached him, and she marvelled at how comfortable he looked in this small domestic space. A space that was hers – or, more accurately, hers and William's. She felt a stab of guilt mingled with something else just outside of her sphere of consciousness. Something intangible and nameless.

"Shift over, Sir, and I'll find it."

He shuffled a little but remained prone against the unit. His legs were to her left, and she could smell the strong musky spice of his cologne. She pulled a brown glass bottle from the cupboard and reached up to the surface where she had placed it. She found herself grappling and wobbling, and her hand briefly brushed against his thigh as she reached up to pull herself upright using the countertop. She felt ludicrous and unsteady. Suddenly, he moved to the other side of the room.

"That should do it," he said, with his back to her as he opened the oven door. "Let me just put these toads in their holes, and then we can sit down and try to make sense of what on earth has happened to your friend."

Chapter Eight: Betty (Now)

"You're early!" Betty cried, opening the front door to Mark. He dropped his bag at his feet.

"I can drive around the block a few times if it makes you feel better."

"Don't be silly." She threw the door wide open and stepped to one side. "Come in, come in!"

He stepped over the threshold and bent down to peck her on the cheek, as was his way. At 55, he still had the same gentle, almost birdlike manner he had acquired as a child, though his dark hair had turned salt and pepper grey.

The door to Flat One opened almost simultaneously with the closing of the front door.

"I thought I heard trouble!" Jonty cried. He jumped straight out into the hallway, one hand out. The two men beamed and grabbed each other's hands, moving into a small but sincere half-hug. "How was the journey?"

"Surprisingly easy. Hence I'm here a bit earlier than expected."

"Yes, Betty and I haven't even sorted the mattress out for you. Such dreadful hosts!"

"Well, let's get you downstairs, and I'll put the kettle on. We can sort all of that out later."

*

Two pots of tea later, Betty knocked on Jonty's door.

"He's just taking a shower, so if you have a moment to help me, now seems like a good time."

"Are you sure he will be comfy up there? You know I was genuine with the offer to put him up at ours."

Even as they spoke, they were making their way up to the first floor, so it seemed Jonty knew his protestation was in vain. Where on earth they'd have found the floor space amongst the knickknacks, furniture, Oxo, and the upright piano, she wasn't sure, but it seemed rude to say, so she stuck with her previous mantra of wanting to afford him privacy.

Paul's old flat was impeccably clean, and he'd not left so much as an old newspaper. The trouble was that it included the curtains, she realised, which were gone. This was understandable, as they were his own. But it meant the bedroom would have been flooded with light every morning.

"I think we should put it here." Jonty gestured to the space where Paul's small dining table once was. "I know it's a bit… peculiar, but he's got great easy access to the kettle here, and there's still a blind. See?" He went over to the window and pulled a chord.

"What kettle?" Betty smiled. "But yes, you are right. This is probably the best spot."

"It feels like a very long time since I saw Mark last." He stared off out the window into the back garden. "Time flies."

"It certainly does. It's been over a year since he came down. Thank goodness for Facetime."

Jonty laughed. "Facetime? I can't even get my mother to even make a call from a bloody landline. Maybe you should show her the ropes. She won't listen to me."

"I'd be happy to."

He pulled down the corners of his mouth in a peculiar frown-come-smile.

"She's… being a bit elusive at the moment. It's been a little while since I got to speak to her."

Betty walked over to him. "Really?" He nodded, continuing to look out. Was he lost in thought or simply evading eye contact? "How long's it been?"

"Ten days," he replied.

"Well, that's not so long."

He pursed his lips together. "It's… it's odd, though. We usually speak a couple of times a week and every Sunday without fail." His voiced sounded far away.

"I see." She crossed her arms. "So that's three or four calls she's missed, then?"

"Effectively."

"I hope she hasn't…." Betty trailed off, thinking better of the words that had formed in her mind.

"Had an accident?" he asked. "Me too. Ben's all for going up there and checking on her, but I'm trying not to overreact. I mean, it is Mum, after all."

He gave a faint, fake laugh and looked her in the eye. His smile didn't reach his eyes, and she noted how they were laced with pink. Bloodshot.

But it wasn't an accident she had considered. What she had almost said – thought better of saying – was that she hoped she hadn't done it again.

*

Ben and Jonty arrived for dinner on the dot of seven with a Tupperware full of cheese and crackers and an expensive-looking bottle of red wine.

"Made yourself at home, I see," Ben said to Mark by way of greeting. Mark was sitting on the sofa in tracksuit bottoms and an old t-shirt, barefoot. He had Oxo on his lap.

"I would get up, but some old stray has settled on my lap." He grinned.

"Don't be too flattered. He does that to everyone… What can I smell? Beef?"

"Lamb chops," Betty replied, half turning to greet them as she chopped salad. "Accompanied by tomatoes from the girls."

"The girls?" Mark asked.

"Ex-neighbours," Ben explained, sitting beside him. "Rosie and Joy. Green-fingered."

Mark nodded and reached over to a glass by his side.

"What's this? Starting without us?"

Mark grinned. "This could be water, for all you know."

"I can spot a Gin and Tonic from ten paces," Jonty said.

"The lime is ready, and the tonic is in the fridge," Betty said. "I have a feeling this is going to be a long night."

*

Mark was talking about Linda and John. It was rare that their names came up, and she often wondered whether this was a good or bad thing. She could feel the tension rise in him as he spoke and feel the sadness, the grief, raw again. She hated it and was inclined to try to move him on when it happened, and yet perhaps that was selfish. He probably wanted to talk. No doubt, he relished the opportunity to bring them to life, even in a fleeting, abstract way, via stories and anecdotes and descriptions.

She forced herself to stay quiet and listen.

"Mum was a straightforward sort of person," he told Ben. "She didn't have any haughty aspirations, and she didn't care about objects, money, or anything material at all. I think she'd have loved to be a completely stay-at-home mum, but she did work for most of my childhood. Not full-time, though. And I was lucky enough to have Aunty Betty to spend time with me." He reached over and squeezed her arm. She placed her hand on his. "Mum just wanted me and Dad to be happy. Everything else came second to that."

"They were so in love," Betty said. "Simple, uncomplicated love. It was wonderful, really. We had a happy little home."

"They lived with you and your husband here, then?" Ben asked.

She felt Mark stiffen.

"Yes, well, in this house. Our house. But William worked away a lot."

"Oh, so it worked out well, I suppose. You'd have been lonely otherwise. You seem to like company around you."

"Wasn't she a machinist at a factory?" Jonty asked, leaning forward to top up Mark's wine and deftly moving the subject on.

Betty nodded. "Ah yes, I remember all the hoo-ha when the Dagenham girls went on strike. People saying they should do the same around our way. Of course, they had to in the end, anyway. Change the pay. But no strikes ever happened. I remember your mother was sort of coy about the whole thing, in a way. Even the talk of industrial action and equal pay. She found it frightfully embarrassing somehow. She didn't mean anything by it; she was just such an unassuming person. I told her, of course, it was right that she should get a pay rise. They gave her a pittance."

Mark laughed. "I can just imagine."

"Blimey. When was this?"

"1968," Betty said. "It seems like a lifetime ago now."

Chapter Nine:
Betty (1968)

At first, she thought it was a part of her dream. The banging. It popped into her sleep so that she found herself imagining she was hammering nails of a sudden. Then, as she stirred, she realised there were also voices. Men. One muffled, one angry.

It was Arthur, yelling at the foot of the stairs.

She jumped up, suddenly alert, and grabbed her gold, quilted robe from the back of her bedroom door. She made her way to the landing and flipped the light switch, peeping her head around the top of the stairs to see what the commotion was below, but she could see nothing bar the faint shadows of someone moving in the dark. She started to descend.

"One last chance!" Arthur yelled, staccato. "Stop now, or I shall call the Police."

He squatted down at the front door, calling through the letterbox, brown and orange paisley print pyjamas open to the waist. Through the speckled, frosted glass, a dark figure loomed outside, periodically hammering on the door. Betty walked up to Arthur, expecting him to jump as she touched his shoulder, but instead, he reached his left arm up instantly, placing one warm hand over hers.

"We have nothing you want here. And now you've woken the whole household. There are women here, for heaven's sake."

"What's… what on earth is happening?" she asked softly.

Fragments of a man's face appeared on the other side of the letterbox, one after another—a jigsaw of a person. An ear, dark hair flopping down, then eyes, wild and frantic, and finally a stubble-edged mouth, wet, grotesque, trying to find its way inside the house.

"Betty? Betty! Let me in. Please!"

"Who is this fool?" Arthur asked, turning towards her. He remained kneeling on the floor, turning so that his face was in line with her belly. His top gaped open, his chest broader than she expected, with short blond hair forming a patch in a butterfly shape from nipple to nipple. She found herself taking a step back instinctively.

"I…"

"Betty. Tell him. It's me! Rob."

*

She filled the teapot when Arthur came into the kitchen, now buttoned up. The ease with which he wandered about her space unsettled her.

"Drugs?" he whispered. He stood just inches away.

"I assumed he was blotto." She shrugged. Drugs hadn't occurred to her.

"Drunk? I don't know. His eyes are like saucers. I'm no expert, but…." He leant back against the counter. "Has he done this before? Does he… does he come around like this?"

She turned to face him. "Absolutely not."

"Good, good."

"I'm not in the habit of having squiffy gentleman callers in the small hours."

"Oh, oh no. That's not what I meant at all. I just…"

She stirred the tea in the pot.

"Would you get the milk, please? Cream jug." Here he was in her kitchen again, though this time, she found herself strangely irritated, and she couldn't quite determine why.

"Gladly." He moved away. "I shall stay, of course. But would you prefer me to get decent?"

"Dressed? It seems to me that it would be pointless at this stage. Besides, it's almost three am."

He didn't answer, reaching past her to pick up a tray. There was that scent again—his spicy cologne.

"I'll do that." She could hear the tightness in her voice. "You go and sit with Robert."

*

When she returned to the sitting room with the tea tray, the two men seemed in deep conversation on the sofa, sat together, hunched forward. The nearby table lamp, with its heavy, pottery base, cast a soft brown light across them.

"Slow down, old chap. I'm not following you."

Robert took a deep breath. "It's far out. Far out."

Arthur turned to Betty and pulled a face. She felt the urge to giggle. They were so unalike, these two men. How had she found herself sitting with them in the half-light, wearing only her nightclothes?

"I beg your pardon?" Arthur asked.

"Have some tea," she said. "Then tell us what's going on."

"Glad you started locking that front door," Robert said, half to himself. Arthur shot a look to Betty, and she wondered if he doubted her previous protestations about not having male visitors at night. "Anyway, I went to see that chick again. At the flat."

"Sandra?" Arthur asked.

"Christine," Betty corrected. Both men nodded.

"She still hasn't seen her, man. Where the hell is she? This is… heavy. She still hasn't seen her. Still hasn't." He shook his head. "Then she said you'd been there. Said you guys had worked it out and that I was the last one to see her. Like I did something, man, she made it sound like it was my fault. Like I did something."

He ended his sentence in a wail, burying his face into his hands. She noted his long, feminine fingers. The dirt beneath his nails.

"Now come on, old chap. There's no need for that."

Arthur glanced at her – eyes wide in alarm. She smiled her reassurance. When he eventually looked up again, Betty gestured to Robert, pointing at the mug of tea she had just poured.

"Sugar?"

He nodded. "Three."

She picked up three white cubes with her tongs, one after another, plopped them into the mug, and passed it to him, followed by a spoon. Then she poured another, this time making it strong, with a dash of milk and just one sugar. She already knew how Arthur liked his tea.

"But what on earth possessed you to come banging down dear Betsy's door at this time of night?"

"I don't know," he answered between slurps. "I wanted to tell her it wasn't me. And I wanted to tell someone about Sandra's funny turns. It was eating me up. I have no one else to tell."

"What do you mean?" She held her own mug between her two hands, enjoying the comfort of the predictable, hard surface and the warmth against her skin.

He leant forward and lowered his voice conspiratorially. "I was asking her, that chick, about the last few days. And she said something about Sandra's nightmares. That was the only strange thing, she said. Sandra had nightmares and had been sleepwalking into her room. Three times she'd done it recently. Said how she was acting wild. Hysterical. I can just imagine. I've seen it before. So I know it would have freaked her out, man. The screaming habdabs."

"The screaming habdabs," Arthur said slowly, announcing each syllable as if it sat awkwardly in his mouth.

"Is this relevant?" Betty asked. "It just sounds like bad dreams to me."

"But it's what she said, man. What that Christine chick says Sandra was shouting. Every time. It's chilling. I can't stop thinking about it."

"Which was?" Arthur asked, exasperated.

"Help me."

Chapter Ten: Jonty (Now)

He was shocked to realise the piano keys were grimy. He had closed his eyes and placed his fingers on the keys, waiting to see where they would take him. He was a few seconds into Debussy's Children's Corner when he had to stop. The stickiness was too much. Usually, he took a soft cloth and a dab of soapy water to the keys at the end of playing. But not this time. They needed wiping before he began.

He'd always kept the lid open, considering himself someone who might feel the urge to touch the keys at any time. And he recalled his teacher, Mr Matthews, telling him that only those who played rarely needed to keep the keyboard closed. Whimsical, maybe, inaccurate certainly, but he had always kept the black and white visible to entice him. Besides, he loved the way it looked. A beautiful black Feurich, it was carefully positioned away from the sun and tuned without fail every six months.

Was that who he was now? Someone who played rarely? How long had it been? He honestly couldn't recall.

Oxo appeared beside him and rubbed against the legs of the stool as he mewed. Jonty bent down to touch him and, as he did so, realised that perhaps the cat was the culprit of the sticky keys. If he and Ben sat together for too long, watching a film or binging a series, Oxo would walk the length of the keyboard in a leisurely fashion before settling down discordantly in a curled heap. They found it endearing and amusing – but he had failed to notice the build-up of dirt because he hardly played at the moment.

Jonty wandered off towards the kitchen and searched beneath the sink for his soft cloth, deftly circling around the end of the sofa and avoiding the floor lamp next to the arch that led to the kitchen as he went. Not for the first time, he wondered if they had outgrown this place. He had stuff. Lots of stuff. And working as he did in antiques and collectables, it was an almost unavoidable hazard of the trade that he was likely to continue to acquire more.

And these were just his personal possessions – at least Ben rarely got to see how full-to-bursting his lock-up was. It didn't look so bad on the website, but in reality, it was overwhelming, even to him.

He filled the washing-up bowl with warm soapy water and a squidge of eco-friendly liquid, dabbing the cloth tentatively and then squeezing off the excess.

But at least it wasn't chaotic, he reasoned. It was clean. It was tidy. Both here and in storage could be described as orderly, even if they were cramped. He knew exactly where everything was; he just found it hard to resist a thing of beauty. And there was so much beauty in the world.

He wondered if he had acquired that from his mother – this desire to hold and own exquisite things. And an ability to see the magnificence of everyday objects. He liked to think they were nothing alike – she was rash, antiauthoritarian, thoughtless, selfish, mercurial, unpredictable. He was steady. Calm. Dependable.

Or at least, he aimed to be: it was a conscious choice, this move away from how she acted. When you have an unreliable parent, you must grow your comfort and strength. Or at least, that's the way he viewed it.

So, when he grew tired of her batch cooking and baking for a week and then forgetting to make food at all the next, he took it upon himself to learn how to cook. He made them dinner every Sunday and Wednesday and Friday without fail from the age of twelve until he left home.

When they moved home three times in eighteen months, and she changed jobs every six, he decided to keep his head down and do as well as he could at school, taking comfort in the routine and predictability.

And when she disappeared for two weeks when he was seventeen, he decided he would never put someone else through the same thing. Never.

He had carefully wiped about a third of the keys, and he needed to rinse and clean his rag, pottering back to the sink, Oxo helpfully in tow.

Not that she was all bad, of course. Far from it. She was exciting, lively, affectionate, expressive, open, frank, intelligent, and much more. Any bold and courageous adjective you could think of would no doubt apply to her.

He could see it now: the edginess, the bravery, the rawness. But as a child, he hadn't wanted quirkiness.

He'd wanted simple pleasures like knowing what time she would be home.

The middle keys seemed the worst, and he was worried for a moment as to whether his usual system would cut through the grime but made a few confident strokes towards him, the length of the keys, and eventually, they started to clean up.

So. He needed to face reality. He was worried. She'd been silent for too long. The phone rang out each time he called, his cousin Louise had not heard from her, and his frankly ludicrous attempt at contacting her by email had gone without reply.

He made one final trip to the sink, cleaned, and then wrung his soft cloth. The water was cloudy and dark. Even Oxo was bored by now and had settled on the sofa, belly to the sky.

The last keys didn't seem as dirty – or perhaps that was wishful thinking. C8 simply received a cursory wipe. He needed this over with.

Jonty dropped the cloth to the ground, sat on his stool and placed his hands tenderly on the keyboard. He took a deep breath.

He would not leave it so long next time before he took it upon himself to play.

Twelve days now. Twelve days since they had spoken.

It was time to go to find her.

Chapter Eleven: Betty (1968)

Arthur had taken leave from work. A long weekend. She had argued against this in a futile and, in all honesty, half-hearted manner, but it was already done, he told her.

Robert had stayed until about four-thirty the previous night, and then Arthur had taken himself straight to bed. She herself had slept so heavily she'd not heard the alarm, waking to the sound of Linda and Mark calling her in a singsong by the side of her bed at eight the next day.

She'd staggered through a day of looking after him: luckily, this was not a day for crankiness or mischief on his part, and – apart from a terrifying twenty minutes before his nap, where he'd screamed himself red in the face – Mark had been happy to eat, colour, and play in his pen with his wooden rattles. This was precisely what she needed; space for her mind to drift and nothing but a series of inane tasks to complete, requiring little brain power. And Linda was finished at four, this time.

Home and smiling by four-thirty. All in all, she was lucky, given her stressful, broken night.

When Arthur knocked on the sitting room door a little before six, she was dozing on the sofa. Ra-ta-tat-tat. Pause. Ra-ta-tat-tat-tat-tat. For a moment, she felt shame. Her mother would have been horrified to know she was caught in this act. But she managed to pull herself to a sitting position before he made it into the room.

"Oh!" he said, clearly realising she was half asleep.

"It's OK." She rubbed her eyes. "Do come in." It was daft to be bashful, given recent events.

"I don't want to disturb you. You need your rest after last night."

She gave a short laugh. "I should think your day has been longer and harder than mine."

He frowned. "Weren't you looking after… your nephew? Sounds pretty exhausting to me."

She considered what he said and smiled. She didn't want to disparage the hard work of childcare or motherhood, but for her, watching Mark was rarely too arduous. Of course, she gave him back at the end of the day – and had plenty of time off.

"He's a darling. But it was a crazy night, wasn't it? Every now and then during the day, it's popped into my head. Sometimes I think he was ludicrous and overreacting. Others, I get a sort of shiver, thinking about… those words."

He nodded, then appeared to think for a moment before gently closing the door.

"I think… something about it all doesn't add up. He was acting awfully guilt-ridden for someone who didn't… who doesn't know anything." He looked her in the eye. "Don't you think?"

"Well, no! Not really. You don't know him. He's a bit sort of dramatic. Expressive. Sometimes, at least. And I think the guilt is part and parcel of the breakup."

"Why would someone feel guilty about breaking up if they knew it was the right thing to do?"

"That depends entirely on the circumstances." She heard the hint of sarcasm, an edge of knowing in her voice, and hoped he hadn't noted it too.

"Well, anyway." He gestured to the space beside her on the sofa. She nodded. "What I came to tell you is that I've booked tomorrow off work. And Monday. It was the right thing to do anyway. I've been a little distracted of late, so they won't mind in the slightest." His eyes fell to the floor. "I could do with not getting up before seven tomorrow…but not just that. More importantly, I think we should go looking. We can take my car. We can spend the weekend out and about, looking properly."

"Oh." The noise was soft and childlike to her ears, but she was at a loss as to what else to say. Anything would be inadequate.

"Nothing, you know… I hope you aren't offended. It's nagging at me. Things don't seem right. I want to help you."

"But where?" she asked. *'But why?'* she wondered.

"Well, at her mother's, to start with." He held his hands up to her, palms flat, before she could object. "I know you said she wouldn't be there, but she might give us a clue as to some other old haunts, boyfriends, relatives, that sort of thing."

Betty nodded. "That makes sense. " She paused. "OK."

"OK?" He grinned, and she watched his shoulders sink.

"I mean, thank you, yes. That's a good idea. Or at least, it's a better idea than doing nothing, which is the alternative." She watched as he slapped his thighs and reached up to loosen his brown, patterned tie before running his hands through his hair. His face was paler than usual, and his chin was unshaven for once. "Oh, but should we ask Nigel to come along too?"

He stopped, one hand on his head, eyes closed, and then he turned towards her. "If you like," he said quietly. "Though the Mini might struggle to contain his height."

He gave a small chuckle afterwards. Insincere but polite.

"Best not, then," she said. "Besides, we want to get going by mid-morning, I expect. He wouldn't be able to get time off that quickly."

They smiled at one another. Everything they had said was true: Nigel would be at work, the car was small, Arthur could do with a break anyway, and Betty wanted to feel useful.

Yes, all of this was true. But there were many unspoken, frightening, exciting, and guilt-inducing facts that were equally true – which they had both chosen to leave unsaid.

*

Up until the last moment, she wondered if the headscarf was a mistake. She'd risen early, dragging her small brown suitcase from under the bed and adding in cigarette pants and a clean top, a dress, underwear, and toiletries. She had no idea where they were staying or for how long. This was both electrifying and terrifying. What on earth would her mother say? Or William? She shook the thought away.

She'd taken the plunge and used her heated rollers that morning. At £17, they were a huge luxury, but before today she'd only tried them once, to ill effect. Then, she'd rolled her hair as tight as she could and waited with fanciful imaginings of glamourous soft waves, but the result had been more Shirley Temple than Shirley Anne Field.

This time, she played it safe and didn't pin them to her scalp with such force. She removed them a minute early before brushing her hair through with her softest brush. A little teasing and backcombing at the back – a couple of bobby pins – and it wasn't half bad. She smiled, then gave a liberal dose of hairspray and tried to calm her racing heart as she viewed herself in the bedroom mirror.

She was just being practical. Curled hair would last a couple of days.

It was still only a little before nine by the time her hair was set, so she had passed the time by changing her sheets and then cleaning the bathroom with gusto. This would be lovely to return home to, she reasoned.

Finally, at about a quarter past ten, she'd popped up to the top floor to visit Linda and Mark. John was at work, but she'd caught him the night before to explain the plan. She'd tried her hardest to be light and brief in her account, but it had been hard to miss the way Linda had shifted from one hip to another and then glanced at John for his reaction. John himself had frowned, then puffed out his cheeks without comment. There was disapproval there, but she steadfastly ignored it.

So it was that she climbed the stairs to the top floor and rapped on the door of their flat. It was Mark she wanted to say goodbye to, in all honesty. But she suspected that Linda knew that. Luckily, she had not been due to babysit, but no doubt she would have seen them all at some point that weekend, as usually happened. They sat, and she attempted to drink lukewarm tea while Mark wriggled in her lap, pulling at her earrings, then her lip, as she spoke,

"It's rather a good job that I don't wear lipstick often." She laughed, leaning forward into Mark's face and blowing a raspberry on his cheek. His giggle tinkled about them in a bubble of glee.

"Your hairdo is fab, in any case. Did you get it set?"

"Ha! I'm relieved you think so. I just had a battle with some heated rollers, that's all. I don't find these things easy." She shrugged.

"You look very nice," Linda spoke quietly, frowning as she did so.

"I thought it would be easier. You know, while travelling."

"I suppose, although those car journeys usually wreak havoc… Oh, I know!" Linda jumped up and left the room before returning with a small, square cotton scarf. "Here." She held it out toward Betty.

"What's that?"

"I use it for work sometimes. In the factory. When I've had my hair done. A scarf."

"Oh!" She considered the proffered goods. The scarf was small, thin, and slightly faded. But it was a thoughtful gift, and she knew that Linda didn't have much to spare, so the generosity meant even more. "No, thank you. It's a good idea, but I have my own. I'll see if I can wrap it around me without ruining this rare attempt at a proper hairdo."

*

And so it was that she found herself with the lightweight scarf her mother had given her a year earlier, wrapped around her hair and tied beneath her chin. It was pink, yellow, orange and delicate: perhaps not intended as headwear. She'd almost torn the cloth when she added her hair pins, and there was still a slight pucker in the nap on one side. But there was really no going back now – for one thing, it had taken a full fifteen minutes to get it into position, and for another, she wasn't sure what the state of her hair would now be beneath.

Arthur's knock cut rhythmically through the silence. She came out from her bedroom, still barefoot, and caught a glimpse of him in the hallway of the ground floor below. She watched as he gave a second ra-ta-tat-tat on the sitting-room door. He held a case in his left hand and stepped from one foot to another, shifting his weight. As he finished knocking, he lifted his hand to his face, pushing down on his forehead as if searching for beads of sweat, before he then lay his palm on his chest, flat and firm. He closed his eyes and seemed to take a deep breath. How small he looked. How vulnerable.

She took three steps back towards her bedroom, pulled the door tight with a sharp bang, and then clattered back towards the top of the stairs.

He was still clutching his case but now smiling broadly and looking up towards her as she descended the stairs.

"Not often I find you in the bedroom," he said jovially. She hesitated mid-step and felt her colour shift but then carried on.

"I'm ready."

"So I see," he said. "Oh, but shoes would help."

She smiled and moved past him to the sitting room. "In here."

"Nice scarf." She could hear the amusement in his voice and didn't dare bring herself to look at his face and see whether she should be flattered or mortified.

Chapter Twelve: Betty (1968)

Linda had been right. Somehow there was a breeze inside the car, even during the first thirty minutes or so of driving when she hadn't even opened the window. Then finally, when she caved – the heavy summer air becoming unbearable – and the draught that rushed from her window to Arthur's felt as if she were utterly exposed to the elements. They may as well have been driving in a convertible.

Such things had never really bothered her. She tried to ignore it— no reason to start fussing now.

The previous evening, she had called Nigel and asked for his mother's address. He'd been taken aback, and for a moment, she wondered if they might argue. He seemed bothered that she was going off without him, almost as if she were interfering or, at the very least, being impetuous – and even more so once he realised Arthur was coming, too. He had been quite frank in expressing that this was a terrible idea. His words were ringing in her ears all day: *"Little Sis, you hardly know the man. Are you sure?"*

But yes. For some reason, she was.

Arthur had given her a map, and they had carefully circled the region of Mrs Ashbury's home in dull pencil lead at her kitchen table. It was her job to help navigate them there. Luckily, Arthur seemed quite confident about the drive. So it was that now she sat with the huge paper document unfolded across her knees and spilling towards the floor of the car in a concertina.

"We'll be at the crossroads soon," he said. "Straight on, isn't it?"

"I… I think so. Sorry. This isn't my forte." She expected him to laugh, but he didn't.

"I don't suppose it's easy when you don't drive yourself."

"True. Also, to be honest, I hardly get out of town. I tend to get the bus or walk within the same five-mile radius." It was only as she formulated the words that she realised this was true.

"You don't go to see your husband, then? William, isn't it?"

She jumped at the mention of him, and the map slid further down. Arthur gazed straight ahead, apparently concentrating on the road, brows low.

"No. Only once. It… it's only a small flat that he has. And his life revolves around work, so it's not what one might call homely."

He made a slight 'humph' sound in acknowledgement.

"He must be quite self-sufficient, though, to be living away. Doing his own ironing and things… though you said he'd never cooked for you. Can't have everything, I suppose."

Had she said that? She couldn't recall. The insides of her palms were growing warmer as she gripped the map across her knees. She felt rather ridiculous, nervous, sweating, holding on to the sheet like a child, waiting for the scary parts of a movie.

"Oh, I don't think he does anything like that at all. I believe he has his shirts dry cleaned, and he eats out or survives on toast."

"Not a self-sufficient bachelor like me, then."

Bachelor? No, he wasn't that at all. It struck her that he was more like a widower.

She heard Arthur take a deep breath, and when he spoke, his voice was raised, higher, louder. "So, do you think you'll ever—"

"Oh, here we are!" she interjected. "The crossroads is coming up. You were right, of course; keep going straight ahead."

She lifted the map towards her face, shielding herself from view, and listened to the gentle exhalation of his breath as it mingled with the breeze of the car.

*

Betty had no idea what had happened to Sandra's father. He was rarely mentioned. But she knew very well the tales of how Mrs Ashbury and Sandra had clashed. Her mother had hoped she would study Classics or History at University and was unimpressed by her choice of Art College instead. For a while, Sandra had survived with minimal financial – or emotional – support. Nigel had escaped the worst of it (sensible and successful as he was), but, in preservation of their relationship, he had never felt able to share with her that he was gay.

Coming close once or twice but ultimately not finding a good time.

"I suppose it would be rather painful in a way," she told Arthur. "Keeping this enormous secret. Not that I would ever discuss relationships or anything of that ilk with my own mother. But this is different because it's part of who he is."

"Isn't your love life part of who you are, as well?" Arthur asked. The words 'love life' hovered in the air momentarily before she answered.

"Well, yes, but it's not like she doesn't know I have… a romantic life. She knows I like men. She knew about William before we married. She can fill in the blanks – accurately or not – to some extent. Mrs Ashbury knows nothing of it, and so she just assumes he's a confirmed bachelor with no interest in anyone at all. Her picture of him is quite inaccurate."

"Are you sure? One can't help wondering if she knows but chooses not to mention it."

"That's almost as bad, isn't it? If she knows but thinks it's too awful to mention." She thought back to that dreadful night last summer when he had arrived at her home, bruised and breathless, having been attacked. "Anyway, she does love Nigel, it seems. He talks about her in a faintly amused but affectionate sort of way – whether or not she either knows or accepts who he really is. But Sandra is a different story. They come to blows each time they see one another."

"Really?" He glanced from the road towards her. "Not literally, surely?"

"No, though I gather there were some shoe-throwing incidents when Sandra was a teen… What

I mean is that Sandra doesn't hold back on her opinions. And Mrs Ashbury doesn't enjoy receiving them."

"Well then," he said with a grin. "I shall look forward to meeting the indomitable Mrs Ashbury."

"Do you know?" She dropped the map to her lap as the reality of their unannounced visit dawned on her. "I think I'm a bit scared!"

Arthur laughed, his head tipped up, broad white teeth on display. "You and me both!"

*

"I don't know why it didn't occur to me that she might be out." She flopped both hands down to her side as she spoke.

"It *did* occur to me that early afternoon on a Friday may not be optimum visiting time, but I had hoped we'd be lucky." Arthur squatted down to peer through the letterbox.

The house was modern though classic in design, a mix of red brick and mock-Tudor features. It stood back from the road, detached, with a meandering drive flanked by several sturdy, impressive oak trees. Betty was surprised to find that the front door itself was up-to-date, painted scarlet red, and boasted three small, horizontal glass windows in the top half – brick-shaped and narrow. It seemed incongruous, somehow.

"What are you doing?" she hissed. Betty had the urge to grab him by the collar of his shirt. He ignored her.

She watched as he reached forward with his left hand, lifting the flap, the pale blond hair exposed on his forearm, his short-sleeved yellow shirt bright and clean in the summer light.

"I want to see if there are any signs of life."

"What... what do you mean?" Her voice dropped even lower.

Arthur stood again, putting his hands in his pockets. How could he be this relaxed?

"Nothing sinister. I just meant that she could be away somewhere, for all we know."

"Right. So... Is she?"

"I've no idea." He smiled, jangling his car keys casually in his pocket as he did so. Then he jerked his head back towards the Mini. "I think we should wait in there. We look rather like we are to sell something door-to-door at the moment."

"Do we? Well, that's dreadful." Betty started to walk back towards the small car, though the thought of returning to its cramped interior did not appeal.

"Avon calling!" Arthur said in a singsong behind her.

Chapter Thirteen: Jonty (Now)

"I've cancelled badminton."

"What?" He was halfway through an email about vintage coupe glasses and could hear the irritation in his own voice.

"We'll go tomorrow," Ben said. "We can get an early start."

Jonty closed his laptop and looked up. Ben stood close, looming over him.

"Sit." Jonty tapped the sofa beside him. "What's brought this on?"

He did as instructed. "Look, I know it's bugging you. You can't fool me. Last night you were sleep-talking, tossing, and turning so loudly that I considered sleeping on the couch. So let's just go. Go to your mum's place. Find out what the score is."

"I know you mean well… I don't know, I—"

"What's the worst that could happen?" Ben interrupted.

But Jonty didn't want to think about the answer to that question. "OK."

"OK?" Ben grinned, and Jonty noticed how he turned towards him, leaning in closer as his shoulders sunk.

"I mean, thank you, yes. Thank you." He took Ben's hands. "That's a good idea. Or at least, it's a better idea than doing nothing, which is the alternative."

"Exactly," Ben said. "And you never know, we might arrive there and find everything's all right. Get to enjoy a trip to the pub and shop at an Honesty Box or two."

"You make it sound like a romantic trip away."

"Maybe it will be."

*

The light still had the soft, grey tones of early morning as they carried their two bags to the front door. Jonty had allowed Ben to pack. They had differing approaches, and this would usually cause some good-humoured ribbing – and occasionally even some bad-humoured bickering – but this time, he was happy to let Ben take charge. While Jonty liked to fold dozens of spare socks and t-shirts into neat packages (better to be safe than sorry), Ben's approach was more haphazard and sparse. No doubt they may arrive with one shirt between the two of them and a loose bottle of aftershave exploded in the centre of a bag, but he was grateful not to have had to think about it.

Jonty paused at the pigeon-holes that held the post for the various flats in the building.

"Hold up." He gave a stage whisper.

"What's the matter?"

"Nothing, I just…."

He dropped his bag from his shoulder to the floor and dug deep into the pocket of his jeans for a slip of paper. He held it up to Ben, who nodded. It was a note for Betty and Mark, explaining they were away for the weekend and asking them to ensure that Oxo was fed and watered. A stab of guilt hit him again. This was probably taking neighbourly favours too far – not even having the courtesy to ask face-to-face –yet he hoped Betty would understand once she saw where they had gone and why.

He felt less guilty about Oxo himself, as Jonty was pretty sure he had a whole battalion of homes he visited to pick and choose his daily meal plan. And if he was lonely, there was always Mark's lap.

*

They had been discussing the Jeep, a common topic of conversation started by Ben. The vehicle was tatty and past its best, and Ben had made it clear he wanted something sleeker as a replacement.

"You know I'd love an electric car, but obviously, that may be beyond our price range. Yes, I know you think I'm a snob—"

"I never sai—"

"You don't have to say it." Ben lifted a hand from the steering wheel in a stop motion. "We have differing tastes… But we don't have to go for a saloon or something with an enormous engine. A Kia or a Hyundai hatchback would be great, as far as I'm concerned."

Jonty winced, and although he couldn't possibly have seen him, somehow Ben noted the silence. Or perhaps it was the way he flinched.

"Sorry… sorry… It's just a big change, that's all."

"Well, you tell me, then. Tell me what you'd like."

Jonty bent down to the travel sweets, balanced in the small glove compartment. "Something with character, I guess."

"What does that mean? Oh, you aren't thinking of some classic car, are you? Or vintage?" Ben groaned.

He passed Ben a sweet, carefully placing it straight into his open mouth. "No, no. I am well aware that would lead to divorce. But something that's not so run of the mill."

"A Fiat? But that's too small for all your goods, surely. You need something with a large boot… Ah!" He slapped the wheel of a sudden, and the sweet almost left his mouth. He laughed and then continued. "How about a Countryman?"

"A Countryman? Never heard of it. What's that?"

"It's a Mini," Ben said.

*

They arrived in Graycott Village a little before midday, having only stopped once, briefly. As they turned into the street, Jonty felt his stomach muscles clench. Neither of them had spoken for the last five minutes of the trip.

Ben drove at a cautious twenty-five miles an hour as they mounted the speed bumps dotted every few metres down the road. Eventually, they were in front of the cottage. He indicated and then deftly parked against the curb in one motion. There was plenty of space. Ben turned off the engine and then reached over to give Jonty's hand a quick squeeze. Then they clambered out of the Jeep wordlessly, leaving their bags in the boot and walking silently towards the small garden in front of her home.

Mum's garden was a peculiar mix of well-tended and chaotic. Giant spiky dahlias rose from large earthenware pots near the gate: discordant pinks and reds. A patch of light blue asters spread alongside much of the short path to the door. But as they approached, he noted the bay trees on either side of the entrance were brittle and dry, and dozens of weeds cut through the overgrown lawn.

This was not wholly out of character, he told himself. She had always been inconsistent in her attention.

He hadn't realised he was loitering until Ben strode ahead. Before he even had time to process what had happened, Ben had banged the door with the bumblebee knocker that took pride of place against the now grey door. He forced himself to catch up with him. He wanted to be standing beside him when Mum opened the door. He wanted her to see him first. He wanted her to know he had made the effort. He was there.

But she didn't answer at all.

Chapter Fourteen: Jonty (Now)

"I did offer, mate. But she didn't want me to keep a key for her. Point blank refused." Steve sounded vaguely defensive – as if he'd let her down somehow.

"Hey, don't worry about it. I know exactly what she's like."

As he was the only one of Sandra's neighbours Jonty knew well enough to speak to, Steve's was the first place they had gone when she didn't answer the door. Now, they were walking across the road back towards Mum's cottage.

"I saw her a couple of days ago, though. She never said she was off somewhere. I don't think she's away."

"A couple of days?" He stopped in his tracks and looked at Steve. "Are you sure?"

"Quite sure. I gave her a bottle of sloe gin."

"Which day? Do you know?" He could hear the edge in his voice; tried to temper it by getting moving again and staring at his feet as he walked.

"Oh, Tuesday?... Wait, no. Sorry. It was Sunday. I'd been down the pub."

Jonty sighed. This was more than a couple of days. Still, it could have been worse.

"How was she?"

"To be frank, she was grumpy and didn't seem to want me to hang about. But other than that, she seemed fine."

Ben was still loitering by the cottage door. Jonty watched him tip a plant pot and lift a doormat, clearly hunting for a key. He stopped as he heard them approaching, standing upright and smiling before extending his hand. Steve looked a little taken aback but then reciprocated.

"Steve: Ben. Ben: Steve," he muttered perfunctorily. "Steve is Mum's jam dealer."

Steve laughed. "Thanks to Nan."

"No luck, I take it?"

Ben shook his head.

"Here, I have an idea. Follow me." Steve walked around the side of the cottage, down a small path with broken slabs. Along the way were an ancient, rusted bicycle, a large metal outdoor clock (no hands), and a folded deckchair. They arrived at the rear of the cottage.

"Good God!" Jonty cried.

His hands went to his mouth involuntarily. The lawn was knee-high at least, flower beds and pots buried in the verdant grass with only their tallest features piercing into view, like shipwrecks. He felt Ben place an arm about his shoulder in a half-hug.

"It's… it's a bit worse than I realised. Never seen it this bad. I usually help her, but she hasn't asked for a while. Didn't realise how long, to be honest…." Steve's words faded away.

"Listen, there's no judgement from me. It's not your job to look after her – or the garden." The implicit follow-up: '*It's mine,*' hung in the air.

Steve strode ahead of them. "Here."

There was a sort of gargoyle on the wall above the backdoor. Even at Steve's (not inconsiderable) height, it was stretch. Jonty watched Steve swing it sideways in an arc against the wall and lift it from the nail beneath. Hanging on the pin itself beneath was a rusty key. Steve took it and passed it straight to him.

"Had a feeling there'd still be one there. Saw her use it one time… Oh, at least a year ago now."

"A gargoyle. How very mum," Jonty said.

"Don't look too closely at it," Steve muttered. "Feel kind of weird holding it in my hand. Wrong, like."

What Jonty had taken to be wood was, in fact, some type of resin plaque with a little figure protruding from the surface. It was grey, like carved stone. Ben frowned and took his arm away from Jonty to reach for the sculpture, which Steve happily placed on his palm.

"Look!" Ben cried. "Typical Sandra."

Steve was shaking his head. "Told you. Dirty, isn't it? She thought it was hilarious, which was my reaction. Used to laugh that I didn't want to look at it."

Used to, he said. She used to.

Jonty looked more closely at the figure. "It's a Sheela-Na-Gig," he said. "To ward off evil from entering the home. Let's hope it's done its job." He placed the key into the lock and turned it.[1]

Downstairs had the faint fug of a home that had been still and stagnant for some time. In the kitchen, as they entered, a few pans sat in the sink, unwashed. A half-hearted attempt to swill them out left them resting with a couple of inches of water inside, curdled and oily with the food remains. The bin was full. Two flies danced about in the air it.

Ben pushed ahead, and it struck Jonty afterwards that this was in protection of him. He feared the worst, no doubt. Steve remained standing in the doorway, awkwardly hopping from one foot to another and clearing his throat.

"Sandra!" Ben called, loud and clear. "It's Ben. Are you here?"

In a daze, Jonty watched as Ben swiftly pushed open the lounge door and took two steps into the room before coming out again. He continued to call out as he took them. He glanced over at Jonty, who was still standing in the doorway to the kitchen, and shook his head once before hopping to the staircase.

Jonty found himself wandering into the lounge where Ben had just been. Even though he'd said it was all clear, he pushed the door open tentatively with two fingers. The curtains were drawn closed, and the room was surprisingly tidy. A book lay open, face down, on the sofa. Nothing much else was out of place. It seemed calm. The warm sun was trying to hammer through the glass of the windows, and the air felt heavy, like an aquarium. He went to

---

[1] *A Sheela-Na-Gig is an architectural carving of a naked woman. Please don't Google if you are faint-hearted.*

the window and pulled open the drapes before pushing the fan light ajar.

"Jonty!" He heard Ben calling from upstairs, the footsteps as he came to the top landing. "Jonty! Come here!"

Something shifted within him. Without thought, he ran to the stairs. One, two, he leapt and made the staircase in five steps, propelling himself with the bannister as he did so.

"Here," Ben said breathlessly as he turned back towards the bedroom, pulling Jonty's sleeve.

They squished together in an awkward jigsaw, crossing the narrow threshold into the room simultaneously. The space was dark and warm. Jonty glanced at the floor, somehow expecting to see her lifeless and stiff. But it was clear. His eyes skimmed the room, back towards the mound of blankets on the bed, where he spotted a small, pink hand, fingers curled over the edge of the bedding.

"Mum?" he cried as he ran to the bed.

She was lying flat, prone, head buried in the gap between two pillows. Her greasy hair lay flat against her forehead, a spot of dribble on her chin. Eyes open. Laboured breath.

"Mum! Oh, my God. Are you OK? Mum!" He grabbed her hand, which remained stuck in the same position, but was at least warm to the touch.

Ben had his phone out. "I'm calling an ambulance." As he spoke, Steve appeared in the doorway, slack-jawed and pale. He didn't speak.

"Mum… what happened?" He pulled the edge of the duvet away from her face and cautiously – unsuccessfully – attempted to lift her head onto a pillow. She didn't answer. "Help's coming, Mum. Ben's here. He's called an ambulance."

A long, low sigh escaped from her as she gestured gently for him to lean in, curling her fingers. He sat on the edge of the bed, trying to second guess where he could rest without injuring her. She looked so fragile. Like a bird. He moved his head closer to her and cocked it to one side to listen.

"Darling… you always make such a dreadful fuss," she said.

Chapter Fifteen:
Betty (1968)

Of all the ways she expected Sandra's mum to arrive, swinging deftly into the driveway in crimson red Triumph Herald was not one of them.

Mrs Ashbury must have seen them before she had even turned in, yet her expression remained unchanged. Lips pursed, she edged her vehicle past the Mini and pulled up immediately in front of the house without so much as a glance in their direction. Then she climbed out gracefully, swaying her handbag as she went, before walking directly to the front door. In her bright pink fitted dress, cat's eye glasses, and blonde hair set, she stunned them into silence.

Betty was confused. She couldn't possibly have overlooked them. And yet there was no acknowledgement at all. She turned to glance at Arthur, who was already striding towards the door, one hand extended.

"Mrs Ashbury!" he called jovially as if they were old friends.

She didn't flinch and continued to look in her bag before fishing out a key, which she slipped into the lock, opening the door in one smooth movement. Only once she had crossed the threshold did she glance their way.

"Well," she said, voice stony. "I suppose you had better come in."

*

"Wait here while I make the tea." She indicated the couch in the front room. They moved towards it swiftly and silently, as instructed. "Not you!" she snapped suddenly. They both looked up, bewildered, but it seemed it was only Arthur this was directed to. "There." She pointed to an armchair nearby. Arthur nodded.

Nigel had warned her of their imminent arrival, she had stated. Betty was unsure if this was a good or bad thing. Mrs Ashbury was clearly irritated at the imposition, but who knew how she would have behaved if they had come unannounced?

The room was large, with a parquet floor. The armchair and couch seemed new – brown abstract flowers swirling over the cream fabric. But the sideboard and occasional tables looked like heirlooms in polished dark wood. The space was immaculate.

They did not dare speak, and for one dreadful moment, when she caught Arthur's eye and he pulled a grimace, Betty worried she was about to descend into uncontrollable giggles; the oppressive silence and the anticipation all conspired to get the better of her. But just as she thought all was lost, Mrs Ashbury appeared again and snapped out of it. She was carrying a metal tray laden with china crockery. She hadn't asked them what they wanted. Placing it down on the delicate table beside Betty, she picked up the small white milk jug and added a generous slug to each of the three cups on the tray. Then she sat down, placing her legs together and sitting with them at a jaunty angle. She dropped her hands into her lap and rested one over the other.

Everything she did seemed practised. Symmetrical. It was rather like ballet.

Momentarily, Betty wondered if she was being taunted – the thought of hot tea after their car journey and wait now seemed very appealing, yet the process had been stopped as soon as it had begun.

"I…" she found herself speaking before she realised what was happening.

Mrs Ashbury raised one pencilled brow and tilted her head. "What is it?"

"Just that I wondered if we could have the tea."

"In a moment, dear. The leaves need to brew, of course." She enunciated the word 'dear' in such a way as to leave no doubt that she meant the opposite.

Betty nodded.

"Mrs Ashbury, we're terribly sorry to have turned up unannounced like this, only we are in rather a pickle. Didn't know what else to do." Arthur's voice was soft and warm.

"I should say Sandra is in the pickle, not you."

"Why do you say that?"

"You ask a lot of questions," she said, voice cold, which was odd as it was really the first question he had asked. Perhaps one question was a question too many for Mrs Ashbury.

"I apologise. We're just concerned for her. Betsy especially, of course."

She ignored him and turned towards Betty. "You're the one with the house."

"That's right."

"Well, Nigel speaks highly of you." Betty began to smile, but Mrs Ashbury pressed on. "But I can't say I was too impressed by your letting rooms to Sandra and that boy. No wonder things have gotten… peculiar. What did the pair of you expect?"

"Peculiar?" Arthur asked.

"The pair of us?" Betty repeated, confused. "Myself and William, do you mean?"

"Who on Earth is William? No, I mean you and Sandra. Egging one another on. You have a hand in this, young lady. All these…" She curved her hand in a royal wave as she struggled to find her words. "Shenanigans."

Mrs Ashbury then got up and moved back to the tea tray, carefully swilling the china pot before pouring three small cups of tea.

It took Betty a moment to comprehend precisely what was being said.

"Me? How is this my fault?" Betty felt a wave of indignance rise from the pit of her belly to her throat. She was being blamed – not for neglecting her or leaving things too long between visits, but simply for being her landlady.

"I'm sorry, I must ask again what exactly it is that we are talking about. What *shenanigans*?" Arthur was persistent.

Mrs Ashbury rose to her full height again, one cup in hand. She took two steps over to Arthur and held it out towards him.

"Goodness, child. Isn't it obvious? Running away."

*

Back in the car, Arthur hadn't even asked Betty to hold the map this time. Instead, he took it from her knees and lifted it close to his eyes, twisting it one way and then the other before placing it back wordlessly. He turned the key in the engine and started to drive.

"Running away was a rather odd choice of words, wasn't it? Makes her sound like a teen rather than someone approaching thirty."

"I rather got the impression that's how she views her. An errant and embarrassing teen."

With a sigh, Mrs Ashbury had told them that Sandra had made her way to Hornsey – North London – as it was the only other place she had any attachment to. She said it with a sneer, referring to 'arty types' and hippies.

"You'll probably find her back with the ne'er-do-wells she was friendly with before. She will be sat in a Public House. But I have no intention of going after her to find out. She'll turn up again when she runs out of funds, no doubt."

At the end of the street, Arthur turned right, heading in the opposite direction from where they had journeyed earlier.

"She may not have been forthcoming as to the reasons why, but at least we have something to go on. It wasn't a completely wasted trip."

"Quite."

"And it did make me wonder…" He drifted off.

"What?"

"Oh, I… never mind. Just an inkling."

After giving them a cup of tea each, Mrs Ashbury had told them how Sandra had indeed arrived at her home unannounced recently, though she refused to be drawn on when batting away their questions with closed eyes and a tight voice.

"It must have been a couple of weeks, though. Weeks ago. Do you think she felt guilty? Is that why she was so… odd about it?" Betty asked, turning to Arthur to see his reaction. She wanted to believe there was a hint of genuine emotion there, even if only one of shame.

"Who knows?" Arthur replied. "But one thing I can say is that she must've been somewhat desperate to turn up at her ma's home like that. Not something I could imagine doing unless one really, really had to."

"I know exactly what you mean," Betty said with an unseasonal shudder.

Chapter Sixteen:
Betty (Now)

She was sitting on the sofa. Oxo, the cat, was meandering up and down, trampling her legs and then Mark's in turn. Mark leaned in towards her, and she realised he was trying to catch the other half of the conversation she was having on the phone.

"Hold on; I am going to put you on speakerphone. Mark's here and will want to know as well…."

Betty took the mobile from her ear and was irritated to find she struggled to see the controls on the screen, turning instantly to the table beside her for her glasses, which weren't there.

"Shall I…?" Mark asked respectfully. She said nothing but passed the phone. Now was not the time to be proud. A few seconds later, the mobile was cradled in his hand between them, the loudspeaker on.

"Go ahead," Betty said.

"A mini-stroke, they think, which is good news in the grand scheme of things. It really could be worse. She's had the flu and hadn't told a soul. That in itself was bad enough, judging by how thin she was. And then this seems to have happened in the last 24 or 48 hours."

"Oh, my goodness. Hence the silence."

"Good job you went when you did."

"Yes, thanks to Ben for forcing my hand. I wouldn't have ended up here if he hadn't insisted." His voice broke at the last words.

"So she's been admitted?" Mark moved the conversation on.

"Oh, yes. She'll be in for a few days, at least. Everyone has been great here, though it took forty minutes for the ambulance to come. Forty! That's not an experience I will forget in a hurry… One minute she'd be awake and lucid, and the next incoherent, slurred. It was frightening. But that was the flu, apparently. Plus, she's dreadfully dehydrated."

"Well, if there's anything you need us to do, just say the word. We can pass on any messages to customers and water plants, and don't worry about Oxo," Mark said.

"Oxo! I'm terribly sorry about that. You must think I'm so presumptuous."

"Not at all," Betty answered. "Now, please text me the address and which ward Sandra is on, and I shall send her a card. I take it she doesn't have a mobile phone yet? I can't talk to her?"

"Ha! No. But maybe I can help her Facetime you in a day or two. Show her how easy it is."

*

Betty let herself into Flat One, placing the post on the table. She made her way to the kitchen, searching the cupboards until she found a jug. It was smaller than she needed, but it would do. She began the process of filling it and then wandering about the flat, watering the dozens of plants one at a time. They dotted the edges of the space, two or three to a wall. Tall, established plants – cheese plants and palms – graced the floor in heavy pots. They had been here all along: she recalled how small they had been when Jonty arrived. How confident and substantial they were now.

She watered these first: feeling the pull at the base of her back as she tilted to reach the pot. Marvelling at how much water they could take.

Next, she looked after the smaller hanging plants. These cascaded down amongst the wooden furniture and could easily be overlooked, so she took her time – deftly nipping off the brown leaves and taking a cutting from the spider plant.

Finally, she watered the graceful aspidistras and ferns, which dotted the tables and the space before the fireplace.

As she worked, she thought back to the time when Jonty had first arrived at the house. She knew him already, of course, but not well. At least, not well as a grown man. He had come back into her life by design: seeking her out and writing to her. An old-fashioned, handwritten letter. Charming. Deferential. Asking if she would consider allowing him to visit her as he would like to hear about his mother's youth and even his early childhood. He had fond memories of summers and some New Year's spent at Hummingbird House as a child. He wondered if she might have any photographs: his mother's collection, and her memories, were sadly wanting, he joked.

But it was more than that, of course. She was certain Sandra recalled a good deal. But she wanted to forget.

And so it was that she called him on the number provided and invited him for Strawberry Shortcake and tea – and found they were surprisingly easy in one another's company. He reminded her of Nigel, though she never said so, unsure how that comparison would land. He began visiting about once a month, meeting up with Mark again on his third or fourth visit. That had proved to be eventful – anecdote after anecdote, ranging from childhood injuries to pranks to broken hearts – leading to a night on Betty's tiny sofa and an extremely sore head for his troubles the next day.

At the time, she had assumed he was planning on using her as a means to find out more about his father. But he had never asked. Not once. Thank goodness for that – because even now, she still had no idea what she would say.

She took a couple of steps into the middle of the room and surveyed the space in a circle, spreading her gaze in a loop about her like a lighthouse. They really had outgrown this place. He had acquired a lot of furniture and knick-knacks – some of which he would keep, and some sell, she imagined.

Jonty's business had blossomed in the last couple of years; not only did he sell directly via his website, but people came to him to hunt down objects for collections or gifts or sometimes simply for advice. He was well-respected in the trade and generous with his time. While he managed to present himself as free and easy – quick to drop things to help her or others, always the first to be sociable – she knew this was only possible because he worked seven days a week to varying degrees. And at times when he did grab downtime, as he had recently seen Mark, for example, he would work into the small hours instead. But he was happy, he assured her. He loved his work. She didn't need to fuss.

There were no more plants to water. Betty walked to the kitchen to replace the jug and then returned downstairs to feed Oxo.

Chapter Seventeen: Betty (Now)

It was Monday evening, and the sky had a soft amber haze. Rosie arrived unexpectedly, burdened with a large bag of apples.

"Goodness!" Betty cried at the sight of her.

"I know you've already had some, but honestly, that tree is out of control. If I see another crumble, I might scream."

Betty gestured to her to come into the hallway of the house. "Let's pop up and see if Paul is there. You know he's a dab hand with chutneys."

"Good call," Rosie answered. Her eyes flit from the post rack to the floor to the stairs.

"Take a breath. You look rather hot and bothered."

"No, no. I'm fine. Let's go up." She walked past her and grabbed the newel post of the staircase. "I could do with the distraction," she muttered.

Rosie bounded ahead, which was rather a blessing, as the thought of climbing all the stairs only to discover the flat was empty was disheartening. It was an annoying fact of life that making her way to the top of Hummingbird House was not a decision she could take lightly these days. It had the potential to wind her or aggravate her arthritis. At least this way, she might get a fair warning not to complete the last flight.

It was a comfort to hear the soft murmur of Mark's radio through the door of Number Two; odd to think of the flats as technically unoccupied. April had only been in the building for a year, and yet her forthright nature had shifted the ambience of the building, somehow. She would often leave her door open and pad in and out of Paul's space throughout the day on the weekends – much to his alarm, at first, Betty recalled with amusement. She used to hear the chatter and laughter cascading through the building regularly before they moved to the top floor. Now April didn't need to leave her door open. And the house was quiet again.

Rosie was already at the top of the final flight of stairs by the time Betty approached them, as predicted. She looked up to see Rosie waiting, looking down at her, a slight frown pinching her forehead.

"Go ahead," Betty called with a wave. "Don't wait for me. See if anyone's in."

Rosie turned wordlessly and raced off again before pounding on the door of Flat Four.

*

"I don't understand why you didn't ring the bell downstairs." April took the bag of apples from Rosie's lap as she and Betty sat on the sofa. "We could have come to you."

"Well, yes, but I wanted to see your new place." Rosie glanced about the flat with a smile of approval.

"Never mind poor Betty," Paul called from the kitchen.

"Poor Betty! I'm not a fan of that moniker. Poor Betty could do with the exercise."

"Apologies. No offence, Mrs W." He walked back into the room carrying two glasses. "Homemade elderflower cordial."

"None for your loving girlfriend, I see?" April teased.

"I only have two hands. If you'd put the tray back in its spot, I might have been able to carry them all at once." He raised his eyebrows at her, then left the room again.

"He loves me, really," April said, flopping onto her armchair. Betty noted that Paul's brown leather chairs had not survived the move.

"Well, this place is adorable. I know you've lost the view, but it has a wonderful vibe. Fab." Rosie raised her glass to indicate 'cheers' before downing most of the liquid in one go.

Paul came back, passing April a drink before perching on the arm of the chair beside her. He leant back behind her comfortably, holding his own drink in his left hand.

April shifted position to nuzzle in closer to him. "Any news from Jonty today?"

"Only a text. Not much change but apparently nothing life-threatening… the poor boy must be beside himself."

April nodded. "He was only telling me about her the other day. She sounds extraordinary."

"Who's this?" Rosie asked.

"Sorry. Jonty's mum. There was radio silence for a while, so he visited her. She lives alone – right little firecracker of a character, she sounds. But it turns out she was bedridden with a virus and complications. She's been admitted. Nasty turn of events."

"Oh, goodness. Give him my love… not that he will remember who I am, I expect." She finished her drink.

"Of course he will!" Rosie had been generous with her time – supporting Ben with his Art History degree on more than one occasion the previous summer. "Come to think of it, you're all arty types. Jonty's mum is, too, right?" April turned to Betty for confirmation.

"Indeed she is. Sandra's very talented."

"Does she paint?"

"Yes – quite abstract and bold. Occasional sculpture too. She has a remarkable imagination. Jonty has one of her old paintings in the flat. You should ask him to show you sometime."

"Cool. She sounds great. I hope she makes a swift recovery." Rosie was playing with her glass, rolling it in her hands. Betty glanced over to Paul, wondering how he would feel about this, but he showed no sign of discomfort.

"Anyway, you've got big news yourself… I want to know about the new place! Fill us in," Paul said.

"Oh, no. Let's chat about something else. I feel like all I ever do is talk about myself these days," Rosie muttered. The glass made a soft chink against her rings.

"Oh, come on. At least tell us how Joy is? Not long now."

"I… let me just get rid of this." Her voice was quiet, with a wobble. Then she stood abruptly and walked towards the kitchen. Betty glanced at Paul, who raised his eyebrows again. April jumped up and followed her out of the room.

"Well… hopefully no bad news… They do say they are some of the most stressful life experiences you can go through – moving house and having your first child. And she's gone through them both at once." Paul spoke quickly and softly, almost to himself. Betty nodded, flummoxed by the scene. She didn't encounter much drama in her life these days.

They sat for a moment in silence, hearing the faint sound of conversation in the kitchen but not the words spoken.

Betty was about to suggest that it might be best if she left – it seemed doubtful that they'd want their eighty-something landlady about at a time like this – when the two women returned again, April pulling Rosie gently back to the sofa by the hand before dropping to the floor in front of her.

Betty turned towards Rosie and gave a soft pat on her arm. Her face was dappled pink and white, eyes wet.

"The baby's fine," she said. "Don't worry. It's not that."

"Is there anything we can help with?" Betty asked.

"Thank you. That's kind. But no… I… you tell them, April. I can't face saying it out loud again."

April sat on her knees, leaning in close towards Rosie. "There's really nothing to be ashamed of, Rose. I told you." Then she looked over towards Paul and Betty. "It's financial. The quotes on the house have come in much higher than expected. And they've just discovered they need a new boiler."

"And the house, the move… I just think I've been dreadfully naïve. And now I'm wondering if I've made a dreadful mistake." Rosie gulped the words in a loud and fast torrent and buried her head in her hands.

"Dear, dear! You mustn't. This is a very stressful time for you. Easy to lose perspective. Try taking one thing at a time," Betty said.

"You have a roof over your head. So what if it's not perfect yet? You and Joy have each other. That's all that matters."

"That's it, though. That's what I'm worried about – keeping a roof over my head. It was tight enough to make the mortgage payments as it was. With Joy not working in the foreseeable, I really don't know how we will be able to pay the bills now that everything is soaring the way it is."

"We're here for you," April said. "We'll think of something." She stood and leant over her, bringing her in for a long, hard hug.

"Can you think quickly, please?" Rosie laughed through her tears.

Chapter Eighteen: Betty (1968)

Arthur had explained that they were less than an hour's drive from Tunbridge Wells, but that was going in the wrong direction if they intended to go up to London tomorrow. Instead, he had suggested they looped back on themselves but bore more northerly, heading to Aldershot or Basingstoke. She had nodded vigorously and assured him this was the right idea, but having been to neither place and unfamiliar with the roads, he may as well have suggested they take Highway 61.

Now they sat opposite one another at one of only two tables in a chip shop. Her fish was greasy and lukewarm, but she found herself eating quickly, grateful for the food. Arthur ate more slowly, chopping his sausage into tiny, hard chunks and staring into space as he held one aloft on his fork.

"Is it good?" she asked.

"Pardon?"

She nodded at his plate. "Is it good? Mine's on the cold side."

"Oh… to be honest, I hadn't even considered it. I'm miles away." He leant forward. "I wouldn't say it's the best."

There was that aftershave again, spicy and sweet.

"I can't believe how easy it was to get a room."

He smiled at her and finally placed the greyish sausage in his mouth.

She'd assumed they would look for a Bed and Breakfast but started to feel anxious as they approached the town, which seemed alive with modern, sprawling developments. For some reason, this wasn't what she'd expected, and she had started to wonder if this town held anything so old-fashioned as a B and B.

They'd had so many newcomers in the last few years that they had even built new sewage works, Arthur explained, leaving Betty unsure what to say next.

What if there was nowhere to stay? But Arthur seemed to know the area and had confidently driven towards the town centre, turning at an enormous bus station towards an area where apparently there were several taverns and coaching houses, as he called them.

They'd tried one, which seemed cosy and sweet, only to find they had just one room left. Thankfully, he immediately dismissed the idea and her fears of any suggestion that he sleep on the floor beside her quickly disappeared.

Nearby, coaching house two had several rooms – it was large and more imposing, with a black and white exterior and Tudor features inside. She imagined it was beyond what she'd have hoped to pay, but this seemed the least of her worries. They had somewhere to sleep for the night. She was more than happy to stay there. And now, dinner to eat.

"We should leave around nine," he said. "It'll take something in the region of an hour and a half, two hours to get there. I would suggest leaving earlier, but we may as well have some breakfast and ensure we get a good rest before heading off again. You know they're planning on building a new motorway in these parts? I can see why."

She picked up the vinegar to try to perk up her chips. All this talk of roads and routes left her feeling useless.

"But where shall we go? We don't even know what street she used to live on. Do you think we should call Nigel?"

"Humph. I did wonder that myself. But I don't really know the chap. How would he take it? I know he's your friend though he didn't seem too impressed with the idea of our little jaunt in the first place, did he? And not putting it too delicately, he rather dropped us in it, with Mrs A."

She shook her head. "I think I've had enough tellings-off for one day. I'm not sure I could face speaking to him… we should head where she said, towards the Art College and get a sense of places students frequent? And if we continue to draw a blank, give him a call in the evening."

"Right-o," he said, taking a swig of his cherryade.

"I'm sorry if this ends up being a wild goose chase. Am I silly, expecting us to march off with no plan like this?"

She wondered, not for the first time, what on earth she was doing.

"Not at all. I was the one who suggested it, wasn't I? Besides, angry mothers aside, I'm rather enjoying myself."

He looked up and grinned at her, and she felt the familiar sensation of blushes creeping like a pink tide from her collarbone to her face.

*

Betty was amazed to find that she slept well: a heavy, unbroken sleep. The room had thick velvet curtains and deep walls, and the warm summer evening had placed her in a cocoon for the night. She struggled to move quickly and was five minutes late to meet Arthur for breakfast.

As she rushed into the breakfast room, she spotted him sitting in the back corner, glancing about the place as he fiddled with a napkin on his lap. She stopped for a moment and took him in – blond hair lighter than ever, face shaved and shiny. He glanced to the doorway and jumped at the sight of her, making to stand with a broad smile. She felt, but ignored, a flutter in her belly.

By the time she reached the table, he had pulled out her chair and moved back to his place.

"I haven't ordered yet, but the bacon and eggs look divine," he said, voice low and conspiratorial. He wiggled his eyebrows.

"Perfect."

He gestured to the maid as she went by and ordered bacon, eggs, and toast twice. "…And tea?"

"A pot of tea for two, if you'd be so kind." He looked to Betty, who nodded.

"How did you sleep?" she asked.

"Not the best, to be honest. When I did drop off, I dreamt I was in detention. I think Mrs Ashbury dredged up some old memories of Junior School." He gave a mock shudder.

"Well, I was out like a light. Ironically, really, given that you were the one doing the driving."

"I should imagine the worry must be taking it out of you."

Worry? She hadn't considered this. But yes, she was worried.

The tea arrived, and Arthur immediately removed the lid and gave the leaves a brisk stir. She noted that the cup and saucer, milk jug, and teapot were each from different sets and smiled. This was all a far cry from yesterday.

"I can't imagine Sandra growing up somewhere like that."

"Is your mother still around?" he asked as he poured milk for her.

"Yes, and as different to Mrs Ashbury as you could imagine. Well, except the sharp tongue."

As soon as she said it, she felt disloyal. It was true; Dorothy was fierce and blunt. Some might even call her a battle-axe. But it was rude to speak ill of your own mother, especially to someone who'd never met her, wasn't it?

"In that case, I think she sounds wonderful," was all he said just as the maid arrived with the food. "Good show!" He declared, marvelling at the plate before him.

He rubbed his hands together. Betty watched: his easy, open movements, his genuine glee. He was a funny, sweet man. A tumble of emotions and thoughts threatened to overwhelm her.

"Eat up!" he cried. "We've got a rescue mission to complete."

*

It was almost 9.30 when they made it to the car; the leisurely breakfast and a short queue to settle up had caused unexpected delays. Betty was unperturbed by this, feeling no rush to dash off to London. For one thing, she'd never visited and was somewhat apprehensive. For another, she didn't know what they'd find – if anything.

After an efficient stop at the garage, where Arthur confirmed his planned route with the pump attendant, they set off towards Haringey, where Hornsey College of Art was apparently based.

"I'm sorry there's no transistor," Arthur said. "Perhaps you could give us a tune?" He glanced over at her briefly with a grin.

"Ha! I don't think you deserve that kind of punishment," she replied.

"On the contrary, I've heard you. Several times. Singing along with the radio or to Mark. You have a delightful voice."

"You haven't!" Her hands went to her face involuntarily.

"I have. And it's been a pleasure each time." His voice was warm and quiet, almost as if he spoke to himself.

"I had no idea the sound travelled so far."

"You look after Mark often, don't you? It seems to be a wonderful arrangement for everyone. They're very lucky to have you."

"Oh, I don't know. I am lucky to have them, too. It's in my interests. There's security in having family at the house… and, of course, I adore Mark."

"He does seem like a delightfully happy little chap."

"He is. At least, for me, most of the time. I have the benefit of not being his mother, of course. A bit of distance for me… and he saves most of the biggest tantrums for Linda."

"You like children, then, I take it?"

She felt herself stiffen, wondering where the conversation might go next.

"I do, I suppose. Though I can't say that I've had an awful lot of experience outside of watching my nephew."

"You're a natural, I think. Ever thought –"

"The turning will be coming up soon, I expect!" she interjected a little too loudly.

She could feel the heat on her skin, her heart fluttering in her chest. Talk of babies would lead to talk of her marriage, she was sure. Babies. Children. How her one and only pregnancy had failed. How she appeared to have lost her husband, too. And how on Earth could she ever explain any of that?

"Five minutes, yet… Don't worry. Anyway, I was going to ask, did you never think of training to be a teacher?"

Chapter Nineteen:
Betty (1968)

It was over two hours before they arrived in North London. Arthur seemed happy to find his way via occasional pit stops where he glanced at the map and then he simply followed road signs. Betty wasn't sure if this reflected well on his knowledge and navigation skills or very poorly on her map reading, but she was glad to be relieved of the responsibility.

They chatted comfortably along the way, him explaining more about his work and a little of his family, she talking about the purchase of Hummingbird House and how she had come to have Sandra and Robert as tenants. Luckily, Arthur seemed happy to accept her story despite the apparent omission of one of the lead characters.

After what seemed like a short while, with a jolt, she realised that they were almost at their destination. Arthur slowed as he came down Muswell Hill. She was surprised to find that the area had the feel of a small town or even a village – not the ominous, aggressive city she had pictured.

"Priory Road!" he declared happily as he crossed a junction and continued straight on.

This meant nothing to her, but she nodded nonetheless. There were relatively few cars. She glanced down adjacent streets, wondering if she might see a sign for HCA, and spotted young children playing in the road – and more than one derelict building from the war still remaining in a heap of rubble.

Priory Road seemed to be a high street of sorts, with a fish monger, a sweet shop, a furniture store, and busy butchers – or was it a cheese shop? – with a queue of women chatting outside, some of whom were West Indian. They passed a Fire Station, modern and bright before a large green park appeared suddenly on the right-hand side.

"Oh!" Betty said.

"Ah… Priory Park, I assume," Arthur said. "I think we could turn off here, but I'd rather take my chances with the main road if you don't mind."

"Not at all." She was mesmerised.

"Aha! Church Lane," he said after a few minutes. He turned right, and the area quietened a little. He continued in silence, leaning forward, brows furrowed.

"So what exactly are we looking for? Any landmarks? Or a street name?"

"Oh, sorry, dear girl." He lifted one hand from the wheel and made as if to pat her thigh, stopping short and instead paddling the air several inches above her leg without making contact. The illusion of intimacy threw her briefly. "HCA is in Crouch End, I understand. South of the park. I've not been here but imagine it'll be obvious as we approach." He gave a chuckle, though she was unsure why.

There was a medieval church, a police station, and numerous pubs to take in as they drove along cautiously, and gradually she noted a shift – posters slapped on lampposts, a young man on his knees on the pavement, sketching artwork in chalk on the ground. Some houses had bright swathes of fabric pinned to the windows as curtains.

There seemed to be more young people here: colourful peacocks of all shapes and sizes, with small clusters on both sides of the road. They sat on the steps of houses or smoking outside of pubs. The women wore mini-skirts and thick, black kohl: some had hair loose and long, falling down in a centre parting – others backcombed and large. Most of the men had hair beyond their collars or brushed forward into their faces, wearing denim jackets or unbuttoned shirts. They were scruffy, open, and loud. Cheerful.

"Surprisingly busy, considering school is out for another few weeks, but I suppose it's because of the sit-in. The fall-out from all that," Arthur said. He was driving even more slowly now, looking about him. "Here we are!"

He nodded towards an imposing brick building that could be seen beyond a wall set back from the road. The front gates were locked, although the wall beside them was low. He pulled up neatly a few metres down the road.

"Sorry… sit in? Have I missed something?"

He removed the key from the engine.

"Yes. Oh, I assumed you'd know, being such a fan of the transistor." He smiled. "There was a huge incident here a couple of months ago. The students took over. Lasted weeks. All-night protests, that sort of thing. It took an age to resolve. I gather the place is still locked up for now. The powers that be and students are 'in negotiations', though the authorities are in the driving seat again."

"I… I thought it was Brighton with the student activism."

"There as well." He smiled. "To be honest, several places. It all started here, though."

"Blimey!" she said. "But why?"

"Oh, I don't know the details exactly. A mix of money and wanting to shake up the curriculum, I believe."

"Yes! I do remember Sandra saying it was surprisingly old-fashioned."

He raised his eyebrows as a young man walked alongside the car, hair wild and curly, framed by large side-burns. He wore an ill-fitting yellow cardigan over an open-necked shirt with wide-legged blue and white striped trousers.

"I should imagine that depends on your point of view." He opened his car door, and she followed suit.

As she stepped out onto the road, she realised how tensely she had been holding herself. Her knees felt tight and stiff. It was a relief to enjoy the fresh air and hear the sounds of the street around her.

"Right then," Arthur called across the roof of the Mini. "I hope you've got good walking shoes on. I suggest we walk down until we hit the next junction. We shall have to be brave and quiz a few strangers along the way." His voice was chipper and light, and he slapped the roof of his car in emphasis.

"I… OK."

Now that they had arrived, the enormity and futility of the task overwhelmed her. This was foolish. Naïve. Like looking for a needle in a haystack. They didn't even bloody know if Sandra was in the area.

But she was here with Arthur, at least. That was one thing for which she could be very grateful.

Chapter Twenty: Betty (1968)

The hair on the back of her neck was stuck down with perspiration. She was glad to have chosen cigarette pants, nonetheless feeling the gentle rub of her thighs against each other as she walked. Her toes felt dusty. It seemed like they had been marching for hours.

Progress had been slow. At first, they had both hopped and hesitated each time they came across someone who looked like a suitable candidate for quizzing, but after fifty minutes or so, they fell into a system of turn-taking and had their patter down to a fine art. Arthur invariably opened with, "*Terribly sorry to bother you…*", whereas Betty began with: "*This is going to sound rather odd, but…*".

While most people were pleasant enough, so far, neither the bothering nor potential oddity had yielded any results at all. No one knew Sandra. No one had seen Sandra. Of course.

"Perhaps we should stop for a drink," Arthur said as they reached a fork in the road.

"That sounds wonderful. But I suspect I won't want to move again if we do."

"True... OK, onwards and upwards. Let's cross onto the other side and make our way back. We can reward ourselves with a drink when we approach the car again."

"Big spender." She grinned at him.

They crossed at the lights, and Betty took a deep breath as they began the slow journey once more. How foolish she was. What a futile quest.

It was late lunchtime now, and the streets were busy. An imposing black building, The King's Head, made the corner, and a mix of working men and students dotted the pavement outside, pints of beer in hand, spilling out from the inn. Smoke billowed from the entrance. She did not regret her suggestion that they keep moving – the noise, smells, and tension of the place engulfed her as they walked by. She noted how Arthur lifted one arm and curved it about her, hovering it above her clothes in protection.

"OK?" he mouthed at her. She nodded. "Should I ask in there, do you think...?"

Given the number of people in the area, it was probably a sensible thing to do. Undoubtedly, it would be just their luck that the one place they didn't quiz the locals would prove to be Sandra's favourite destination. But she didn't fancy the idea in reality.

"I... I suppose so." She glanced further up the road. "Hey! But no... There!" She was gabbling, struggling to find the words. "Look!"

Arthur dropped his arm onto her shoulders and steered her away from the throng.

"What is it?"

"There… We should try there." She pointed, jabbing the air. "The Buttercup Inn."

*

Betty had rushed ahead of Arthur, striding urgently towards the pub. She pushed open the heavy double doors and found herself in a small, dark space. The air was thick, warm, and heavy. It hit her hard, a contrast to the outside. She slammed to a halt, rubbing her face, eyes prickling and dry, struggling to adjust to the dim light. The place was close to empty – two male students sitting together, huddled at a table, one older man cradling a pint at the bar. It was almost silent – a far cry from The King's Head.

Arthur appeared behind her. "But what makes you so sure—?"

He stopped suddenly, then pushed past her shoulder, jogging towards the back of the pub, uncharacteristically brusque. Betty was still standing, stuck to the spot she had hit on arrival, disorientated and woozy.

"Betsy! Come on!" He was calling to her as he made his way quickly to the rear of the room through a fug of smoke.

She shook herself into action, blinking rapidly and then moving once more. She was headed to the back of the pub where he now stood. She could just make out the shape of him, hazy and dark, alongside a pillar, a table lamp, and a booth. And Sandra.

Chapter Twenty-One: Jonty (Now)

He sat next to the bed. Her thin hair fell flat against her forehead: streaks of white amongst the salt and pepper grey. Her skin had always remained remarkably youthful – especially given that she decried the benefits of any form of skincare regime or beauty treatment. Sandra had used nothing but olive oil soap for years. Until recently, she could easily have passed for ten years younger, her complexion matching her boundless energy.

But now, he noted, small patches of eczema formed about her eyes, desiccated and sore, and a large brown mole protruded on her forehead, crusted. Ominous. Had it always been there? He couldn't recall. The skin below her jaw, once soft, was now papery and crumpled. Her lips were thin and dry. She looked every inch her age.

A nurse came towards the bed, wheeling a Blood Pressure monitor. She stared into space as she approached, casually dancing the machine about her. They seemed to prod, press, and monitor Mum hourly – not that he wanted to complain about this. He was glad of the supervision. It just seemed odd how it happened wordlessly, robotically. Tablets appeared in miniature cups, and she was instructed to take them with no explanation of what they were. Urine samples were tested. Blood Pressure was taken. All without any comment as to why.

The nurse smiled at him as she stopped beside the bed. "Will you wake her, or shall I?"

"Depends on how brave you're feeling. She'll let you know if she's unhappy about it." He smiled.

"I do have a name, you know." Sandra's voice came to them, thin and broken but still vivid. The nurse jumped and then gave a little "Ha!".

He looked down. Her eyes remained closed momentarily before she flicked them open and fixed him directly with a squint. Jonty couldn't help but laugh.

"Sorry, Mum."

"Anyway, what on earth are you doing here? I've already told you to get packing."

She tried to shuffle herself into an upright position, batting away the assistance of the nurse who waited patiently beside her.

"I'm here for you," he said. "I want to help."

Chapter Twenty-Two: Betty (1968)

"Sandra?"

Her eyes remained focused on the glass before her, though she must have heard and sensed their approach.

"Sandra! We're… we're here for you," Betty said. "We've come to help."

There was no indication she had heard them at all.

Sandra had a large table in a square booth. She was in the middle of an old pew, facing the door, gazing into space. On the table before her were two empty glasses; the third in her hand was less than half full. A crumpled, empty cigarette packet was next to the ashtray, ashes from smoked and half-smoked cigarettes forming a miniature murmuration of grey across the wood.

Betty sat in a vacant chair at the table opposite her. Sandra's thin hair fell flat and greasy against her forehead: Betty noted for the first time the beginnings of salt and pepper grey about the temples. Her complexion was pale – small patches of eczema formed about her eyes, desiccated and sore. She wore no makeup. A cold sore cracked her upper lip. Was she prone to them? Betty couldn't recall. She looked older. Exhausted.

"Sandra?" Betty said again quietly, unsure what to do. Sandra flinched.

She wanted to bundle her up in a hug, but instead, she reached her hand over and touched Sandra's forearm, which was surprisingly cold. She could hear Arthur move in the space behind her, feel the pressure as he leaned on the back of her chair.

Without warning, Sandra flicked her eyes in their direction, looking from Sandra to Arthur and back again before fixing her directly with a squint.

"What on earth are you doing here?"

*

Arthur returned to the table with two half pints of mild, placing them in front of her and Sandra before returning to the bar for his stout.

"H... How many have you had?" she asked.

Sandra didn't answer, her shoulders jolting before she flicked her eyes and curled her upper lip in disapproval. Clearly, this was at least her fourth. But it seemed equally likely to have been more. The table was high, damp, and messy.

She had barely spoken since they arrived, mostly acting as if they were not there at all; except, alarmingly, it did not seem to be an act. She jumped each time one of them spoke and had only once made eye contact. The rest of the time, she sat staring down at the table, swinging one foot briskly, banging it against a table leg. The swift regular beat as her toes crashed against the wood was alarming – Betty wanted to grab it, hold her still. And she could see a tiny, rapid tremor within her, throughout her body, jiggling her greasy hair and the black and white geometric earrings tangled within it. She wore a loose shift dress.

"Well then," Arthur announced as he approached, placing his pint down next to Sandra's drink and making to sit on the pew beside her. There was little room. "Budge up, dear girl."

She did not acknowledge him. He persisted regardless, and for one worrying moment, Betty wondered if he'd end up balanced half across the seat and Sandra's right knee. But she watched as he deftly, softly, tenderly pushed against her slender shoulders and simultaneously wriggled his hips back and forth until he had carved out a space for himself. It was a confident move. Natural. He smiled placidly the entire time.

Eventually, they were wedged in together on the bench: Arthur, with a faint benevolent grin on his face. Sandra with a tight forehead and slight scowl. Both faced Betty.

He picked up his pint and took a deep swig before releasing a satisfied sigh.

"I needed that. Thirsty work." He took another sip and gestured to Betty to do the same, angling his pint glass towards hers. "Come on, Betsy. You must be in need, too."

"Betsy," Sandra said faintly, quizzically – almost imperceptibly.

Betty looked at her, confused, but Arthur did not react, so she picked up her glass as instructed. It didn't make it to her lips. She had no idea how she could swallow.

"Sandra," Betty said quietly. Sandra started and then looked up at her, head still down, staring up from beneath her heavy brows and a few oily strands of hair that were stuck to her face. "Sandra," she repeated.

"What?" her voice cracked.

"Look at me." She paused. "We've been looking for you. We were worried."

Sandra looked down at the table again. There was a long silence. Betty felt it fall, thick and damp, across them all.

"You trying to make me feel guilty? Not sure I have room for that alongside this bloody nausea and banging head."

"What? Goodness, no."

"Don't be silly old girl," Arthur said. "But you did ask."

"Pardon?" Sandra asked. She turned towards him slowly. Despite their proximity, it was as if she was noticing for the first time. "I didn't. I didn't ask for anything. I… I didn't want any of this."

"'What on earth are you doing here?' That's what you said. Well, that's your answer. We're here because Betsy's been worried about you… Truth be told, I've been rather troubled myself."

"Why?"

He took another sip, and Betty found herself following suit, the harsh, bitter liquid forcing a wince.

"Because you disappeared off the face of the earth without telling a soul where you were going, that's why."

Sandra frowned and looked away again. She placed her left thumb in her mouth and chewed. Betty noticed the raw quick, tiny specks of blood dotting her skin like a spray of paint. The nails of her hand were each ripped down to their beds.

"Stop calling her Betsy. Man, it's bloody annoying."

"Goodness, I had no idea," Arthur answered jovially. "Sorry about that." He looked to Betty and gave a quick wink. Heat splattered her neck and lower face in an instant.

They all sat in silence. Betty wanted to speak but was at a loss. Eventually, surprisingly, it was Sandra whose voice punctured the silence.

"How did you know where I was?"

"We spoke to… a couple of people. This area seemed to be the only place you had any real connection to."

Sandra scowled but did not meet her eye. "A couple of people? Who were these 'people'?"

"I… just Robert and Nigel, and, well…."

"We've been to see your mother. Charming family home you have." Arthur downed the remains of his drink.

Sandra leant forward swiftly towards Betty, cradling her own glass between both hands. "You went to see my *mother*?"

"I, we…"

"Now, now. You didn't really leave us with any choice. Your flatmate had no idea where you were. Nigel – delightful chap, by the way – he drew a blank. And that ex-boyfriend of yours was dreadfully worried but not exactly full of answers. So a trip to see Mrs Ashbury was our only option."

"You went to see my mother," Sandra whispered. Betty looked up to see her staring at her, eyes glassy and damp.

"I'm sorry." The betrayal hit her in a wave. Of course, she would have been humiliated by this. The last thing she would have wanted.

"She doesn't think much of your ex-boyfriend, I gather," Arthur said. "Has she met him? Will she?"

Sandra snorted.

"Didn't approve of any of it, I should imagine. You two."

"That's an understatement. Especially… especially now. Obviously."

Arthur nodded, though Betty was unsure whether he truly followed her. Perhaps he was humouring her. Everything Sandra said seemed somehow disconnected. As if whole sentences and paragraphs were missing from the conversation to enable her to piece the true meaning together.

"She'll have told you then. So you know."

"Know—?" Betty interjected.

"Yes, she told us how you are *in a pickle*," Arthur interrupted. "That's how she put it… But you must let us help you. That's what friends are for."

"A pickle," Sandra repeated.

"I'm sure it seems insurmountable right now, but honestly, dear girl, you can get through this. You're not on your own."

"But that's just it. I am. I am on my own."

"What does… he say? That chap? Sorry, I've forgotten his name."

"Who?" Betty asked, confused.

"Robert," Sandra and Arthur both said at once. Betty jumped as their voices doubled in unison.

"I haven't told him."

"Ah," Arthur said. "Well, drink up and then we'll make a plan. We can discuss it in the car on the way home."

"I… I don't think I can. Besides, I don't even… I don't even know what I'm going to do yet. I can't see him. Not yet. I can't."

Sandra picked up her drink and downed it in one go, glugging back the lukewarm contents. Betty stared at her gullet as it contracted up and down in time with the sound of her swallowing. Then Sandra lifted her fingers and roughly combed them through her dank hair. Even now, half-cut, exhausted, dishevelled, something was captivating about this girl. Even now. She was transfixed.

"I know you can't see it now. But we will work it out," Arthur said.

"Will someone tell me what's going on? Tell Robert what? Do what?"

"Darling," Arthur said gently. *Darling. Darling Darling.* She felt it echo within her to the beat of her heart, and she watched as he lifted his left arm and placed it delicately across Sandra's shoulders. "Sandra is pregnant."

Chapter Twenty-Three: Betty (Now)

Back in Jonty's flat for the third time, it struck Betty that it was possible that Jonty and Ben might never return. She placed the parcel she had just signed for on their table. A hollowness filled her belly. Of course, it was bound to happen at some stage – that they'd move on – and yet it was not something she'd ever considered.

She sat, pulled out her mobile phone and snapped a picture of Oxo seated on the lower keys of the piano. She sent the image to Jonty with a winking emoji.

In the flat now. All fine. Let me know when you plan to return, and I'll get you some bits and bobs.

She was fishing, but she needed an update. Reassurance. Besides, she wasn't entirely convinced she'd been given the full picture of Sandra's health.

She stood once more, finding it dangerous to be still for more than a few moments at a time these days; settle for five minutes, and it could stretch to thirty, as once the stiffness set in, her motivation to move dwindled. She would not want to get up again.

Betty walked to the window, opening it a crack, before going to the kitchen to search for cat biscuits. Her phone pinged.

Thanks! I'll give you a call this evening.

Great – we are going to the cinema early eve so free 8.30/9. x

Mark had planned to stay around five days, but a week had passed, and he was being vague about his departure date. In an effort to make his stay more worthwhile, she'd suggested a trip out. She worried how much of his holiday he was using up and how sympathetically his workplace would view an unexpectedly protracted stay. Still, he brushed off her concerns with a laugh, saying this time off was long overdue. Not that she was complaining. She cherished the time she got to spend with him, now as much as ever.

She also hoped for at least one more evening where he and Jonty could be together – she suspected he did, too. In fact, a gathering of all the residents was long overdue. Even having that one extra floor between her, April and Paul had created a strangely muffled quiet, a sense of distance that was not there before. Yes, a get-together was on the cards. She could include Rosie and Joy. Perhaps a barbecue.

*

"I'm not saying it was bad, exactly. Just…"

"Not your cup of tea?" Mark grinned at her as he unlocked the front door. They'd been to see the film – a two-hour action feature that seemed to have been shot with all the lights off.

"I know, I sound terribly old-fashioned, but it was hard to see what was happening – and I wish they'd enunciate!"

He opened the door and stepped aside to let her through. "I'm with you on that. The cinema is always both extraordinarily loud and indistinct. Sometimes I think I'd benefit from captions."

"Wouldn't we all?" Betty asked, moving down the corridor to the door of the Basement Flat. It still seemed odd to her that there was no sound emanating from Number One -- no sound from the floor above.

Her landline started ringing as she took the stairs, but much as she wanted to, she couldn't risk rushing. Luckily, the caller – presumably Jonty – was persistent.

"Betty speaking," she said when she finally reached it.

"Hello there! I thought I might have been too early for a while."

"Jonty! No, well.. we are just walking through the door. This gives me an excuse to have Mark make a pot of tea for once." She smiled at Mark, who nodded in acceptance and went to the kettle.

She sat and began an awkward tussle with her chiffon scarf. The evening had been warm, and she'd been coatless, unusually going out in just a cardigan and a small wrap.

"Well, I must send Ben off to do the same. *You have to beg for a cup of tea around here*." These latter words were louder and pointed, and she pictured Ben mirroring Mark's eye-rolling and dutifully padding off to the kitchen.

"Where are you staying?" It occurred to her that she'd never asked.

"Oh, at Mum's. We were in a cheap and cheerful hotel for a few nights, but it seemed like a waste, what with her place being empty. Besides, I wanted to get a sense of the place. The maintenance, whether it's watertight, safe, that sort of thing. She's never exactly been one for health and safety."

"Does she know? Or do I need to keep this unannounced inspection secret?"

"Goodness, yes. I wouldn't dare just move in. She knows we are staying. We are under strict instructions not to touch anything, mind you."

"I don't blame her."

"Speaking as a fellow fan of clutter, I heartily agree. Much as it's tempting to bin the random skeleton leaves and pebbles dotted about the place."

"It's in your genes," Betty said. Mark placed a mug of tea beside her on the occasional table, along with a saucer of biscuits. "Anyway, please bring me up to speed, won't you? Any news? Any change?"

Mark sat beside her as Jonty talked her through the last few days. Periodically, she would stop and relay some information to him. Sandra should be out on Monday, she explained. The doctors were pleased with her progress. After that, it was a case of resting up. Yet Jonty was concerned about her living alone. Very little food was in the house when they arrived, and the washing was backed up to the point that her wardrobe was almost empty. Sandra was refusing point blank to have any discussion around homecare – and as she had capacity and no history of falls, there seemed little they could do to override this.

"But she's clearly not coping like she did. Things have slid… there's a stack of bills and paperwork knee-high in the hallway, and she'd have had a choice between a 1990s cocktail dress or vintage kimono if we hadn't come along and done at least five loads of washing," Jonty said.

"I should imagine she has friends, though. She was always a social animal."

"Yes, some… but I've been disappointed by how few people have been to see her since she's been admitted. She's only had two visitors that I'm aware of. And it seems her closest friend, Marg, is… no longer with us. She didn't even say."

"That's a dreadful shame. I find it's the company that helps to keep me young these days."

"And action films!" Mark called as he returned to the kitchenette to top up their tea.

*

Betty was surprised – and frustrated – to find herself awake after midnight, although she'd been in bed since a little after ten. The conversation with Jonty had unsettled her, bringing home the brutality of ageing. In short, it seemed Sandra could no longer be left alone. Sandra: vivacious, independent, feisty as she had been for so long. Perhaps Betty should pay her a visit? But even then, what use would she be? At 83, she was hardly in the position to act as someone's carer.

And it was troublesome to watch Jonty slide into the role of protector in their relationship. He'd often been cast as the sensible one; that was true. Cooking, calming Sandra down, and acting as a rudder to steer their little unit through any storms or difficulties. But Sandra had still made her own decisions; she had her own mind. Strong opinions. She pictured him there, folding his mother's bedding and tidying her kitchen. Checking the sell-by dates on her herbs and porridge. She would hate for Mark to do the same. Hate for him to have to.

There had been times when Sandra had needed help, of course. More than once, she had disappeared or packed up her life: 'running away', her mother called it. There was the time she'd handed her notice in at the bakery and put all her possessions in boxes in a friend's attic, not telling anyone she had a new boyfriend and was moving counties until they all received an invite to their housewarming through the post. And she had travelled to Portugal once, not letting anyone know where she was until she'd been missing for about twelve days, perhaps longer. Betty couldn't recall what had triggered that one. But Jonty – poor Jonty – he had only been a teen, left alone to take himself to school for his A Levels, unsure if he'd ever see her again.

On the surface, it was terribly selfish and an extraordinarily irresponsible way to treat a child. Cruel, even. But there was a fragility in Sandra. She was like a delicate pane of glass, mottled with a spider's web of hairline fractures. You might not notice them at first. But they were there. She was never too far from cracking.

Chapter Twenty-Four: Betty (1968)

Sandra had moved into Betty's bed. Betty had been worried they might suggest some sort of bedroom-sharing arrangement; usually, that would have been fine by her, fun even, but the parallels with her own fleeting experience of pregnancy were too stark. Besides, Sandra was still having nightmares. Screaming, chaotic, petrifying ones. She worried Mark would hear them.

Betty wanted to support her wholeheartedly and was more than happy to feed and clothe her. But just one year earlier, the tables had been turned. And the emotions this new twinning brought were unexpected and raw. She was terrified for Sandra in case she lost her child. Terrified for Sandra in case Robert didn't want to keep it. And sad: painfully, excruciatingly sad for herself, which seemed self-centred and inappropriate given that Sandra was clearly struggling.

Sandra had stopped washing. Her hair had flattened into one oily piece that no longer moved, and a musty haze hovered about her. It had taken two days to persuade her to remove the shift dress they had found her in – in between, she slept in it or padded the house with her pale bare feet hardly making a sound. She had barely eaten. The tips of her fingers were raw, red, and bloody, and the hollows beneath her eyes a peculiar pale blue-grey.

No one had spoken to Robert, though Betty had, at least, called Nigel. Sandra hadn't responded when she had made the suggestion, and Betty had taken that as a lack of objection. He had come straight around the day they returned, within an hour of the call, but Sandra had been asleep – or pretending to be.

"I'm going to call Nigel again," Betty whispered to Arthur. They sat at his kitchen table, eating the cheese sandwiches he'd made for supper. It was five days since they'd returned.

"I think that's a good idea."

"Really? I was worried you'd think I was overreacting."

"Not at all." He put the remains of his sandwich down and met her eye. "I was wondering if we should get the doctor around."

"But… well, there's not an awful lot they can do at this stage of… at this stage, is there? She must only be a few months along. Is there a dreadful rush?"

"Betsy, dear Betsy," he said, leaning forward. "I didn't mean for the pregnancy. I meant for her mental health."

"What? No! She'll be OK. She's not… crazy. She's just upset and confused. And sleep deprived."

"I didn't say she was 'crazy'. But she's skin and bone; you must have noticed. And she honks to high heaven. For someone who was always so impeccably put together, she's hardly recognisable. That's more than just a bit of upset. I… I've seen it before. A family member." Betty felt her eyes fill; she didn't think she could speak. "Listen." He took her hand in between both of his. "It's OK. I'm not saying she won't get better or that it's the end of the world. I don't think she, you know, needs institutionalising. I just think she's unwell. We all get ill sometimes. We all need help."

Betty nodded. "Let's try Nigel first."

"Of course."

"And persuade her to have a wash," she said between tears.

*

"She's in the bath now," Betty said. "Thank goodness. I had to be quite forceful. But Arthur, well, he made me see how bad it was. Last night, over supper. I think I had my head in the sand a little. So today, I've been like a dog with a bone. She finally relented, just to shut me up, I think." Betty held the phone close to her mouth, wondering how far her voice might travel.

"I had no idea things were that bad," Nigel said.

"Well, why would you? I wasn't keeping it from you exactly, but I think I thought her… appearance was sort of circumstantial. She'd been crashing on the floor of an old friend's house, and they weren't the most salubrious surroundings. I had no idea it was intentional. Or an issue, at least."

"But I take it it's not just the washing thing? She's not herself?"

Betty sighed. "No, she's not. At first, I thought it was a lack of sleep. And quite frankly, she seemed irritated by our meddling. Cold shoulder, sort of thing. Now I think… I'm not sure exactly. She's disconnected. I'm talking to her, and it seems like she's there, and sometimes I think she hears me, she understands, but it's as if she's behind a thick pane of glass, and the words aren't getting through. I can see her, but she's barricaded away."

"Hmm… rather like a painting of her," he said.

"Like a ghost."

*

The bath seemed to have perked Sandra up, enough to eat the fish in parsley sauce Arthur had knocked up for them. She even had a little potato.

It was good to see her finally dressed and no longer wrapping Betty's dressing gown around her. Betty had laid out an outfit of cigarette pants and a yellow blouse on her bed while she bathed and had been mortified to discover that, despite her tiny frame, Sandra could not close the zip. She was starting to show. In the end, she had replaced this with a babydoll dress that swamped her and hid her burgeoning bump in its folds and paisley pattern.

Arthur cautioned her not to read too much into this sudden improvement, stating that a bath and a piece of cod weren't enough to turn her around completely, but Betty couldn't help but feel optimistic.

"I know, let's put the radio on," Betty said, returning to the living room where Sandra clutched a cup of sweet tea. She pressed the button, and 'Mrs Robinson' filled the room.

"I wondered how long you could last without your blessed radio," Arthur teased. "It was noticeable by its absence."

Betty laughed. She was about to counter with a comment on his dancing when the doorbell rang. They both frowned. This was odd. Most of her visitors went straight into the hallway before tapping on her sitting room door. Nigel had done this earlier in the week when he visited – why should he start ringing the bell now?

"For John?" Arthur speculated as he walked towards the door. "Or Linda?"

Of course, Linda and John might have a visitor, though this in itself would be rare. Betty followed, loitering a couple of steps behind as he opened her door and made his way to the hallway.

The last time someone had come to her front door uninvited, it had been Robert, so she was relieved, momentarily, to see the faint outline of two people through the frosted glass. They were in a heated discussion, and their words, loud yet indistinct, could be heard through the door: a man and a woman. Arthur leant forward to the latch just as the door burst open.

"I don't care, mother. She won't be expecting us to stand on bloody ceremony." It was Nigel, red-faced and agitated, directing these words to Mrs Ashbury.

Chapter Twenty-Five: Betty (1968)

They sat awkwardly in the sitting room; Nigel next to Sandra on the sofa, Mrs Ashbury in the armchair, and Betty and Arthur a little apart, using the dining table chairs nearby. Betty was glad of the distance, especially as she had seen how little time Arthur had left the tea to brew before pouring – she'd been about to correct him when he had looked up, locked eyes with her, and winked.

"Once more, can I say how sorry I am that my mother has taken it upon herself to descend on you like this?" Nigel broke the silence. "For someone who prides herself on manners, she can be shockingly forward."

"Needs must when the devil drives," Mrs Ashbury said. Her voice was quiet and curt. "Goodness, it's dreadfully warm in this room."

"August has snuck up on us," Arthur offered. Mrs Ashbury twitched at his words though she made no effort to turn around to look at him.

"It's also August in Sussex. But we open windows there."

"Mother!" cried Nigel. He turned to Betty apologetically. "I knew this was a bad idea."

"You were rather short of good ones, though, sadly… And honestly, I'm glad I came. Look at the state of her." She gestured in Sandra's direction with her cup and saucer.

"Thank you very much, Mother." These were the first words Sandra had spoken since Mrs Ashbury arrived, and there was a slight ripple across the room as she did so. Quiet, fragile, and tiny, she looked like a child. And a terrified one, at that. But her voice still held grit in it.

"Well, honestly, darling. That dress is fooling no one. And you don't have a scrap of makeup on, do you? A little blusher wouldn't go amiss."

"I think that's the least of her worries," Arthur said.

"Do you?" Mrs Ashbury said pointedly, finally turning to acknowledge the man at the back of the room. "Well, *I* think it's none of your business."

To her surprise, Arthur laughed. A sincere, loud laugh which he accompanied with a slap of the thigh before shaking his head gently.

"It's no laughing matter," she muttered before returning to her drink.

"Look, I can't speak for Mother, but I just wanted to check you were well. And coping? It's all been a big bloody shock, and I gather you haven't had much rest and food lately. You need to look after yourself."

Sandra shot a look at Betty. "Been gossiping again?"

"It's not gossip," Nigel said, taking her free hand in his. "We all care about you."

"All of you?" Sandra glanced up at Mrs Ashbury.

"Don't be silly, darling. Of course, we do. But we must get on with things and face reality. Moping around in your silly friend's house wearing silly clothes isn't going to change anything—"

"Hey!" Arthur interjected.

"—so you must come home with me. We can go this evening. It would be better than the daytime. And you can hole up there for the next… six months? No, I'd say four, actually. Until it's time. And then we can all move on."

"What on earth do you mean?" Nigel said.

"Yes. Please explain," Arthur followed up.

"Oh, you do fuss. She can come to me, and I shall look after her. Home-cooked food. No one to stick their noses in. It's terribly quiet there."

"We can all move on, you said. How can Sandra move on? She'll have a baby, Mother. This isn't some Spanish holiday we're talking about. It's pregnancy."

Nigel was still clasping Sandra's hand while she stared into her lap. She was withdrawing again. Pulling away. Betty could see it on her face – the distance, returning.

"She can't possibly keep it. I rather think that's obvious."

"What?" Nigel cried. Sandra flinched. Arthur made to stand, then stopped himself, hovering above his chair, unsure of his next move.

"Now, steady on there, Mrs Ashbury. This is Sandra's life we're talking about here. She's the one who should be making the decisions, don't you think?"

"No," she said. "I do not. She's done a dreadful job so far. Besides, this is out of her hands. It's what's best. I have contacts through the church. I've already put feelers out."

"Out of… out of my hands?" Sandra said, pulling her hand away from Nigel and staring down as she flexed her fingers.

Mrs Ashbury tutted and placed her cup and saucer on the table beside her.

"You must give it up. Surely you see that." She leant forward towards Sandra, speaking slowly and loudly. "Obviously, it would be better if you came to that conclusion yourself – and there's time for all that. You'll come around. Come to see that it's the only option."

"The only option," Sandra repeated.

Betty felt a wave of agitation come over her. Before she knew what she was doing, she'd come over to her and squatted down on the floor in front of Sandra, sitting on her knees as she had so many times with Mark in this very room.

"You have plenty of options," she said. "Listen to me. Plenty. You must do what is right for you. No one can force you to do anything."

"On the contrary, I think you'll find I can. She's unmarried, with an inadequate income, and a fragile mental state. And I'm her mother. I would prefer her agreement, but it's not required. I'm certain that the Moral Welfare Workers at the maternity hospital would agree with me."

"The Moral… honestly. What are you talking about?" Arthur banged the table with his fist. Betty glanced over at him. "*Sorry*," he mouthed.

"I would prefer it if you didn't take that tone with me. I'm looking after her best interests."

"I think you should leave," he said. His voice was deep and firm.

"Oh, do you? Who exactly are you, anyway? The lodger from the Basement Flat? Her landlady's fancy man?" Betty winced. "You have nothing whatsoever to do with this. Perhaps you are the one who should leave."

"On the contrary," Arthur said. "I have a good deal to do with this. I'm the baby's father."

Chapter Twenty-Six: Jonty (Now)

The car journey back was tense. Jonty was racked with guilt to be leaving his mum, and Ben's blatant delight to be returning home was grating on him. The jeep bounced along at speed as Ben sang along to 'Hey Jude' on the radio, tapping the steering wheel rhythmically as he did so.

"You could at least pretend to be worried about her," he snapped.

"I have been worried. I *am* worried."

"Really? It doesn't look that way. It looks as if you are delighted to see the back of her."

Ben took his eyes off the road briefly to glance in his direction.

"Mind—" Jonty said, tapping the wheel.

"I am worried… But I am also worried about my job and our cat. I am also worried about our life. And you! I'm bloody worried about you!"

Jonty winced. "I'm not the eighty-something who's just had a mini-stroke."

"No, but you are exhausted. And besides, this whole thing has taken it out of you. You can take a horse to water…."

He was right, of course. The endless battles with Mum over homecare and Day Centres – even getting a cleaner – had been wearisome. She relented on nothing. She wanted nothing. But he knew she needed it: the company, if nothing else.

He was tired. Fed up. Ben was right. He took a deep breath, knowing that what he was about to suggest was likely to cause a row but not seeing how he could avoid the topic.

"There is one thing we could consider for her. I know we've always said we couldn't live with her and—"

"Oh God, Jonts, please don't. We've had this out before." Ben's jaw clenched as he changed into fifth gear. The car struggled with the unwarranted gear shift and began to stutter and hop. Ben revved the engine and attempted to steady it.

"No, no. Don't worry. I'm not going to suggest she comes to stay with us. We don't have the space for a start."

Ben snorted.

"But Hummingbird House… well, there are two empty flats there. And obviously, there's Betty. And plenty of people around…" Ben dropped his head melodramatically, pretending to headbutt the steering wheel repeatedly. "Just… just think about it, would you? It's an idea, that's all."

"There has to be a better solution," Ben groaned.

"If you can think of one," Jonty said, "I'm all ears."

Chapter Twenty-Seven: Betty (Now)

There are moments in life that remain etched in your memory. Betty found that, even now, she had the same tidal wave crash over her whenever she thought of those words, "*I'm the baby's father.*"

That one simple sentence. That one devastating moment came back to her a couple of times a year – this time, it had resurfaced at the thought of Rosie and Joy. She had no idea who the father of their baby was (and no intention of asking), but the idea that there might be some third party around to help them during their time of financial crisis had come to her while she was pottering in the kitchen. And then unwarranted, unplanned, Arthur's voice had come to mind.

"I'm the baby's father."

Rosie and Joy would have considered the baby's biological father and his contribution if appropriate. It was ridiculous to think otherwise. Besides, they were unlikely to want to be rescued by a sperm donor or to make demands of him, which it appeared likely he was. But she was hoping for a solution for them. Rather like Arthur had provided for Sandra.

She'd spun internally at his words that day and felt herself collapsing in on herself like a black hole. The sensation came back to her again. The folding. The falling. That day, she was on the floor and yet somehow unsteady. Sick. Confused. She couldn't look at him. Couldn't look at her.

And yet, of course, he wasn't the baby's father. That was an impossibility. Sandra was showing – she was at least four months pregnant. Arthur had met her once, only one month earlier. One month to the day. Besides all of this, this was not something he would do. Not Arthur. Not her Arthur.

Yet it had taken her the best part of ten minutes to process this fact, some of the worst moments of her life. And in the meantime, a scene had unfolded around her quickly after he said it. She had sat in the middle of it, and despite her devastation, her confusion, she could still recall every word. Nigel accepting the story, or perhaps cottoning on (she was unsure to this day) and stating firmly that this changed everything. Sandra was no longer a single mother. Arthur had rights too – more than Mrs Ashbury.

The two men came together, taking charge of the conversation. There would be no more talk of adoption – forced, consensual, or otherwise. Arthur wanted to keep the baby, as did Sandy.

Sandy, he called her. *Sandy. Sandy. Sandy.* Betty felt nauseous. Sandra did not speak.

And then Mrs Ashbury was standing. She moved over to Arthur at the table, stood still and regal before him, and seemed to take him in for the first time. Betty thought she might slap him for a moment, but then she simply said: "Better than the hippy, at least." And she left.

Arthur and Nigel were demob happy then. Betty recalled Nigel slapping him on the back as Arthur offered him a beer, the two men standing close together, grinning, laughing, and congratulating one another.

"Why did you say that?" Sandra's voice cut through their jubilations. It was at this moment that Betty's thoughts came together, and she began to climb out of the hole. She looked at Sandra, who was frowning and still. "Robert's the father. You can't be the father. You aren't."

"Dear girl, I know that. It's not the immaculate conception. But it seemed like a good solution and … well, it worked, didn't it?"

"That's a cruel game," Sandra said.

Arthur baulked. "Goodness, why do you say that?"

"She has to find out sometime. And your little joke won't be funny when she does. I'll be back to square one but with a pack of lies to justify her low opinion of me."

Arthur walked over to Sandra and sat down in the space Nigel had just vacated. Betty remained on the floor before her, taking in the words they each spoke. Unsure what to think or feel.

"Sandra," he said. "Please. It wasn't a joke. It's not a game. And she doesn't need to find out."

"But how?" Betty asked. "And… and why?"

She could still recall how her eyes had stung: *don't cry. Don't cry.* She told herself. And somehow, she had succeeded.

"I wanted to help. Both of you. I couldn't stand… If Betsy thinks highly of you, that's good enough for me." He was staring at Betty. Earnest. Sincere. This strange, kind, open man. "So, if you do want to keep this baby… I'm not suggesting we get married or play happy families. We can work out the details. But one thing's for sure; you can use my name. Tell everyone I'm the father for all I care. The midwives. Your mother. The – what did she call them? – the Moral Welfare Workers. All of them. Hell, I'll even sign the birth certificate."

And he was as good as his word.

Was he a knight in shining armour? No. Ultimately any awards for bravery or strength went to Sandra. But it was 1968. And his support made the battle substantially easier.

*

Jonty and Ben had finally returned. Betty had left eggs, milk, coffee beans and bread for them and resisted the urge to knock on their door as soon as she heard them return. After a while, she heard Ben's voice singing goodbye to Jonty, which she assumed was a sign that he was going for a run.

Shortly after this, her phone pinged.

I have Bakewell tart. There was a thumbs-up emoji.

She laughed. *Sharing is caring.*

Ready in five?

Ready now!

Sure enough, less than five minutes later, Jonty rapped on her door and then made his way down the steps. He held a tart on a plate aloft, carefully balancing it as he took the steep stairs.

"Honestly, Betty. If I didn't know how much it annoyed you when people mentioned it, I'd suggest you consider moving into one of the upstairs flats."

"Luckily, you know better," she said.

He came over and kissed her cheek. "Any movement on getting new tenants?"

"A vague possibility of a young man. He's coming to view Number Three on Tuesday."

"Young? How young? Can he afford it?" He took the plate to the kitchen counter and opened the cupboards in search of plates.

"Now, now. Don't be so judgemental. He's a legal secretary, apparently."

"Fancy! Even legal secretaries look young to me these days. And what about Number Two?"

She noted an edge to his voice. A deliberate casualness. "Oh, no news. I can't say I've exactly been trying too hard to fill the place. I even wondered if I could afford to leave it empty. The thought of new tenants… well, they shan't be the same as the old ones. What if it doesn't work out?"

"Better the devil you know? I may have a suggestion for you, actually," he said.

*

The following Saturday was to be Mark's last night, so she wanted the barbecue to be a success. And luckily, everyone was free and keen to get together. Even David – Dai – was coming along. She'd made a Strawberry Shortcake and prepped a salad. Mark had taken her to the local butcher and then stopped by the greengrocer to collect aubergine and corn-on-the-cob for the vegetarians.

"Waste of a barbecue if you ask me," Mark quipped.

"Don't you dare say that in front of the girls."

"I'm joking! When have I acted like a caveman?"

"In that case, you can prove your connection to your feminine side this afternoon and help me prep the veg and salad."

"At your service, ma'am," he said. She would miss him.

Evening soon came around, with Ben, April and Paul being the first guests to arrive. Betty took a slow and careful walk to and from the kitchen, bringing plates, crisps, salad, and drinks out and ignoring all offers of help. April and Paul took their spot on the wooden bench, and she smiled as she noted how he placed his arm tenderly across her shoulders in his familiar way. The warm heavy evening held the faint song of a blackbird in the distance.

"Hey," Paul asked. "What's going on with Number Two?" He was staring up at the window above them, where the indistinct shadow of a person could be seen moving about on the other side.

"Ah," Ben said, with a smile, "Don't you know about Betty's new tenant?"

"What? No! When did this happen?"

"Hey, no fair, keeping us out of the loop!" April declared. They were both squinting in a futile attempt to get a glimpse of the tenant.

"One moment." Ben held his mobile phone up and pressed a button to speed dial. The phone was on loudspeaker, and Betty chuckled as she saw the confusion on April and Paul's faces. Finally, Jonty answered the call.

"Jonty, I'm in the garden with our lovely neighbours, and they are just wondering who it is that's taken up residence in Number Two. Perhaps you could enlighten them?"

"Of course. One moment." There was a mischievous tone to his voice.

April and Paul looked quizzical, staring at Ben and his phone until the air was punctured by a cry of "Hello there!" from above. It was Jonty – waving to them all from the window of Number Two.

"Ha!" April said. "What? I don't understand…"

"Wait, you two haven't…." Paul drifted off.

"God no," Ben said. "This is basically a very elaborate man cave."

"Fancy coming to see my new pad?" Jonty called. He was leaning out the kitchen window, beaming broadly.

"Nah, I hear it's a dump," April called. "The last tenant was a right messy bloke."

"Cheeky!" Paul laughed.

"I'm disconnecting you now," Jonty said into the phone. "Come into the garden, or we shall all talk about you behind your back."

"So, has he actually rented it, then?" April asked Betty.

"He has indeed. He's decluttered Number One, and he's using Paul's place – Paul's old place – for storage and work. They'd outgrown the flat, so it seemed like a perfect solution for everyone."

"Can you do that? Don't you need a change of use application or something?" Paul asked, ever practical.

"All in hand," Ben answered. "Besides, if we get stuck, I hear there's going to be legal advice on tap in the near future, too."

"Really?" April asked. "What's this? I feel like I have missed out on all the gossip lately."

"Come inside and help me finish plating things and I shall be more than happy to fill you in," Betty replied.

*

By the time David appeared, Jonty and Paul had already lit the barbecue coals, and the group were on their second bottle of wine. The evening air was cool, but heavy with the scent of jasmine. Betty sat amongst them for once and listened, conceding that all the prep was done and food in hand. The chatter of her tenants and ex-tenant fluttered about her like birdsong, and she allowed it to wash over her.

April was telling Paul and David about the solution the girls had come to – how awful it had been to see Rosie in despair over the finances and the way the house had proven to be a money pit with issue after issue and some unscrupulous contractors involved to boot. But things had worked out perfectly in the end. It could not have been better. They had a lodger moving in. Not only that, but she was an artist.

"And you'll never guess – oh, but there they all are, now!" April cried suddenly, half rising from her seat.

They looked over at them all in unison: Rosie, Joy, and their new lodger.

"Hello, Sandra," said Betty, and smiled.

Epilogue:
Arthur (1984)

He watched as she pottered about the kitchen, moving from one surface to another, piecing together her signature Strawberry Shortcake. She had placed the berries in concentric circles and was now dusting the finished cake with icing sugar. He took in the sight of her as she concentrated, watching her beautiful, earnest face through a soft haze of sugar. Then she was done. She turned towards him, smiling.

"Oh! I didn't know you were watching me. I feel daft now."

"Any excuse to stare. You know I can't take my eyes off of you."

She waved her tea towel vaguely in his direction. "Stop embarrassing me."

He rose from the chair and moved towards her, dancing with jazz hands and two left feet. She blushed, as she always did.

"Well, the wait is over," she said. "It's ready."

There was a pause. She didn't meet his eye, but he felt his flesh tingle as she placed one arm loosely about his waist. She squeezed him.

“Really? Ready?” He took a step back to look at her face. “Are you sure, Betsy?”

She nodded.

“I’m certain,” she said and kissed him.

*

Already missing the tenants and their neighbours? A short story from the Hummingbird House series; coming in November 2023. Pre-order your ebook now.

About the Author

Jane Harvey is a pen name. 'Jane' crafts fun fiction for the thinking woman, where she enjoys exploring unexpected friendships and writing happy endings. This is lucky because, in real life, her (prize-winning) fiction is a little bleaker.

She was born and raised on the island of Jersey, where she also works for a mental health charity.

Enjoyed Searching for Sandra?
Please leave a review.
You have no idea the difference this can make.

Historical Note – Forced Adoptions

Between 1949 and 1976, an estimated 185,000 babies were removed from unmarried mothers for adoption in England and Wales, either via coercion or with 'permission' given by the child's grandparents, with none sought from the mother.

Many of these women were teenagers, often giving birth in church-run 'mother and baby' homes. This practice did not end until responsibility for processing adoptions was moved from the voluntary sector to local authorities in 1976.

In 2022, a Joint Parliamentary Committee on Human Rights conducted an Inquiry into forced adoption. They concluded that these mothers were subject to cruel and inhumane treatment, with long-term psychological harm for both the women and their children. This included the intentional withholding of pain relief during childbirth to 'teach a lesson' to unwed women, the instant removal of the baby without warning at birth, or delays in receiving treatment, such as stitches, for blood loss.

Amongst other recommendations, the Committee called on the UK government to make a formal apology. Both the Catholic Church and the Church of England had apologised for the practice prior to the Inquiry.

In its response in March 2023, Boris Johnson's government acknowledged that what had happened was wrong – but declined to issue an apology.

Acknowledgements

Thank you to my early readers: Mary, Lily, Julia, Sara-Jane, and Cheryl. Thank you to Dave for casting an extra eye over the London sections.

A special thank you to all the readers of Book One who encouraged me to keep telling the stories from Hummingbird House. There are more to come.

ALSO BY

Dreena Collins

Jane Harvey is the pen name of Dreena Collins.
Dreena also writes literary fiction.

And Then She Fell – a Suspense Novel

Wish Bone and Other Stories (November 2023)

Embers (Tales of Courage and Comeuppance)

She Had Met Liars Before – Six Very Short Stories of Strength and Survival

Taste: Six of the Best (Six Readers' Favourites from previous works)

Collected (The Complete Stories: The Blue Hour Series plus Bird Wing)

Bird Wing (A Flash Fiction Collection)

The Day I Nearly Drowned (Short Stories Vol. Two)

The Blue Hour (Short Stories Vol. One)

Printed in Great Britain
by Amazon